AWAKENING THE
SUN QUARTZ FIELDS

AWAKENING THE SUN QUARTZ FIELDS

A Novel

By Pamela Camille

iUniverse, Inc.
New York Lincoln Shanghai

Awakening the Sun Quartz Fields

iUniverse, Inc.

For information address:
iUniverse, Inc.
2021 Pine Lake Road, Suite 100
Lincoln, NE 68512
www.iuniverse.com

Cover Artwork by Kurt F. Smith

ISBN: 0-595-31582-8

Printed in the United States of America

I lovingly dedicate this book
To my beloved family,
Reed and Willis and Walt.
You are simply the best,
And your love is my light.

Contents

AWAKENING THE SUN QUARTZ FIELDS

From the Earth Memories Archives
Compiled by Marla, Sea Faerie Keeper of
Memories

It is said in India that when you learn the truths about former lives, you are "lifting the veil." The veil is diaphanous and sweetly hued, possibly the color of pink pearls, but when lifted, the heart soars, and the soul can at last find its purpose. Colors become crisp and vibrant, and light radiates as never before. The souls of ancestors who have gone before can sigh with joy, for when the veil is lifted, their spiritual progeny can at last move beyond limitations, and ultimate destiny can be fulfilled.

This is the story about the former lives of this planet, and members of a clan who lived through many of them. It is the tale of a series of lives and civilizations that changed the course of countless others. Indeed, the course of the entire planet has been changed by the various civilizations' flowerings and deaths: it is the timeless recycling of wisdom and folly through the ages that has brought us to this pivotal moment in the life of planet Earth.

This tale spans six millennia, but its origins reach back to Earth's first flowering, in the Motherland of Mu, to a family with fan-feathered brows. The veil shrouding their power and light has darkened their destiny for six thousand years, and that is too long a time. As I free this tale, sending it into the light, I feel within my being their ancestors rejoicing.

Their story begins long after the wild earth's gaseous core had exploded, ripping apart our Motherland, Mu. Mu was our hallowed, verdant island continent, the "Empire of the Sun." My original home of Mu, or Lemuria as it is sometimes called, was shredded 13,000 years ago. Of its grand vastness, only mere atolls and spits of rock on the Pacific Ocean remain of its physical land.

Sixty four million people perished when the gaseous tunnels beneath Mu that had clogged over the millennia finally exploded. We who survived as Ascended Masters learned the sad, hard way humans must learn: when we forget our history, mass destruction always results.

We who love Earth and her people most, and who remember the ways of a united heart, mind, body, and spirit have stayed on, through the millennia, to guide Earth to her final triumph. That is, we are hopeful this will be her final triumph. The only other possibility is her final destruction.

I get ahead of myself, as I often do. It is hard not to, when one has dwelled in the River of Life for thirteen millennia. I often digress when reminiscing of my first homeland, but it is not without relevance, for the Clan of the Fan-Feathered Brow can trace its ancestry back to the Motherland. This, as you will see, matters a great deal, and connects the Clan, ultimately, with all of us.

I return to my swift sketch of the historic period preceding the Clan of the Fan-Feathered Brow. Three thousand years after the destruction of Mu, our sister-island continent in wisdom and commerce, Atlantis—the Red Land—suffered a similarly violent end. Massive earthquakes and volcanoes were followed by waves of water high as the mountains that once stood on her. Ravenous waves swallowed her whole. (Atlantis was a newer land, and mountains, after all, are a new phenomenon. We had no mountains on Mu; we could see across her lush plains for hundreds of miles. Across the miles, our splendid temples jutted proudly toward the island sky.) Great segments of the Atlantean population had also forgotten their history, bringing about her destruction, but the Ascended Masters of Atlantis preserved her energy. The Apache and the Sioux carried her red soil and her ancient knowledge of energy to the "Land of Promise"—what would later be called America. The Ascended Ones have patiently waited for this very time to unleash the powers of light from Atlantis. The story of light that is to transform Earth and her people is part of the later chapters, and, indeed, very central to the history of the Sun Quartz Fields. For now, this brief, historic introduction of what came before leads us to the story of the first bearer of the fan-feathered brow, several millennia after the sinking of Atlantis. I begin:

More than six thousand years ago, in the land of Egypt, a child runs, laughing, from the river Nile onto its loamy shore. The child is eight, with long legs browned by the sun. Her black, almond eyes are ringed in kohl. Her glossy black hair slaps against her bare brown back as she runs. Her face is lit with the joy she takes in the freedom and power of her body with every swift, vibrant move.

The tall, dark priest who watches her is frightened by her beauty. Her beauty will destroy him, someday. But the girl is oblivious to all that is dark. She runs laughing from an ibis who has chased her away from its nest. The ibis frantically flaps its wings as it wobbles toward her, but the girl respects the mother bird's right to guard her progeny. Stifling a giggle at the large bird's awkwardness, the girl retreats.

A shadow darkens the space, and the girl notices something from the corner of her eye. A shudder rushes through her. She whirls in time to see a crocodile's long, narrow snout drifting purposefully toward the nest of the ibis. The girl grabs two stones from the bank and hurls them at the crocodile with strength that startles her. The crocodile retreats slightly, but is still intent on destroying the family of the ibis. Without thinking, the girl flings her body onto the scaly beast, thumping its narrow head. Snapping its jaws, the crocodile withdraws beneath the muddy water of the Nile.

In later years, the girl would remember only a flash of white light, and the sense of being lifted. She would never forget the experience: the bright light, the lifting of her body into the air, and the warmth of the fluttering wings surrounding her. Ancient knowledge flashed through her, warm like the rushing of the many wings. As her body and spirit flooded with bright consciousness, she felt surrounded by hundreds of the sacred birds. Countless midnight-glossy Black Ibis wings flapped, glinting in the sunlight. Loud and powerful, the charcoal-black wings belonged to giant birds with deep, black eyes that looked inside her. Long revered as Defeaters of the winged serpents who once flew into Egypt on breezes from Arabia, these birds softened their flapping before disappearing completely. One ibis remained, and the girl knew her instantly as the mother ibis whose eggs she'd rescued.

The mother ibis was white-winged, but her head was dark and shiny. The very tips of her wings were gray and black, but the softness and purity of her blinding white wings were what the girl would remember, and that memory would be passed onto generations after her, down through millennia. Her life as a seer began then, when the holy mother ibis proclaimed her Nanu—Guardian of the Light that comes from the Sky Goddess Nut.

Without having to think, as if in a trance, Nanu performed the first Mother Ibis ritual. She sank to the ground. On her knees, she took some loamy soil from the bank, and with her finger, drew Egyptian hieroglyphic symbols that came to her from within herself. Resembling a child's sun drawing, and a long, sideways-pointed ibis beak, in her language, she wrote "Mother Ibis". She then tossed dried reeds on the symbol, and lifted her arms to heaven. Immediately, the reeds began to burn in a small, fragrant fire. She felt soft feathers surround her as she was lifted. As she hovered above the flames, she saw frightening visions: strange places ripped apart by earthquakes, and glowing rocks in the heavens. She was viewing her clan's future, which raced before her.

Memsek, the tall, thin priest watched all. He shook. Despite the glimmering heat above the Nile, he felt cold in his lone darkness. He watched Nanu's face fill with light as the spirits of the birds surrounded and buoyed her. Memsek's amber eyes were aflame with the color of the desert sands at sunset. In them, too, was sorrow: sorrow over what would come, for he already knew he faced both eternal love and eternal darkness in this one, bright child.

"Aton, God of Sun, and Nanuk, God of Night, I place my destiny in your hands. Please, Gods, help me."

Nanu would later remember that the next transformational event of her life was the Dream of the Otherness, which came just before her first menses. The nights were still cool, with the Nile's slight breeze smelling fresh and green as she drifted into sleep. The dream was troubling, bewildering, and filled with bizarre foreign images. Whereas her first, mystical experience with the ibis family—where Light and Knowledge had come in the form of all things familiar to her—nothing in the Dream of the Otherness was familiar.

She was sleeping, that night, when a strange-looking bird, unlike any she'd ever seen, held her in its warm, feathered breast. Its hold on her was firm, but its breast fur was softer than anything she'd ever felt, and she nuzzled into it, not completely unafraid. The softness of the fragrant, white and brown-speckled feathers intoxicated her, and the great bird's heartbeat spoke to her. While she felt her body sway in a drumbeat-heartbeat trance, the owl (she would never know that bird's name, "owl," nor would she ever see it in her lifetime, except in dreams) lifted her.

Nuzzled in the warm, soft, breast feathers that surrounded her like a coverlet, she flew above Egypt, and all that she knew. It was a glowing, golden land, canopied by vast numbers of stars that lit the desert. She looked down and gasped at the beauty of her home from above. They flew for what seemed a long time; her face grew cold.

Her body remained warm, deliciously so, and she curled her body into the breast feathers. Even her feet were warm, tucked up into the soft, white and brown-speckled feathers.

They flew over an alarming landscape, filled with jagged, hard-looking peaks shaped like the pyramids of her homeland. (She had never seen, and would never see, mountains in her lifetime.) They disturbed her, with their cold, white-snow tops, and their jaggedness. With such arrogance did they jut toward the sky! Clearly, they were Gods. The trees surrounding the bottoms of these mountains were also foreign to her. Pine trees, something else she'd never see in this lifetime, looked nothing like the graceful date palms of her home. These trees seemed human, in both shape and spirit; indeed, they leaned toward the mountains above, in a clearly worshipful pose. She could feel the power of their love for these high, rocky peaks. The great bird had taken her to a place filled with Gods of great power, whose holy subjects below, existed solely to pay homage.

"Why are you taking me to these strange places, to see these strange things?" Nanu's heart asked the owl's beating heart. The answer came in a rhythm, which she felt drumming into her.

"Within you, there must be a memory. You must carry this memory within you, in your DNA, to pass onto your great-grandchildren, for this place is the destiny of your clan."

The owl's great, vast eyes somehow appeared before her like huge, yellow suns, and she felt lost in them. Deeper and deeper into them she fell, floating, swirling. The glowing golden heat of those great, wise eyes filled her. Wisdom: she felt that word, and felt the essence of it enter her. The owl, Caleina, radiated light and love. Nanu felt Caleina's light and infinite love fill her, for one rich, eternity-filled moment before she woke in a start, hearing a flapping sound.

The fluttering of soft, strong wings left her as she gained consciousness. Caleina was gone. She shook herself, trying to return to this time, this place. She went to wash her face in cold water. In the water's reflection, she saw her face, and gasped.

She pulled away from her reflection in terror. Her heart drumming loudly, she looked again. Above her eyes, her own eyebrows—the eyebrows she'd had yesterday, or whenever it was, before her dream-flight to distant places—had been removed. In their place were feathers, in the shape of a small, papyrus fan. Dark, beautiful, feather-soft fans arched above her eyes, bewitchingly. Indeed, a thousand men would soon claim to be "bewitched" by the beauteous Nanu, "of the feather-fan brows."

I, Marla, have written this story because I am the Sea Faerie Keeper of Memories. I look back on Nanu's life with nostalgia, thinking how young I was when Nanu won her feather-fan brows. We who live in Koba, the watery underworld in the River of Life, know all that happened to Nanu, because we chose her. Since the time our beautiful island continent, Lemuria—the land of Mu—exploded and sank, thirteen thousand years ago, we have looked above and chosen the keepers of our seeds, our love, and our wisdom records.

Sixty million people went to their watery grave when Mu finally sank. I am one of the few spirit-faeries Queen Rona decided could stay through the millennia—this is my thirteenth—as the Keeper of Memories. I record and plant memories in the hearts of a chosen few. Nanu and her descendants have been chosen, just as Memsek was chosen to thwart her and her descendants through the millennia, so the Clan could learn the Ascension lessons. From those Egyptian times, he has always appeared as some sort of nemesis to Nanu's descendants. His motive—power, and the desire to control others—will always be the same, and still is, at this critical moment of approaching battle with the Greed Kings.

I have lived lives above, through the millennia, and have enjoyed my different lives in different lands. I enjoyed holy India, cultural Daughter of Mu, where I lived as a poor woman. I was the caretaker for the Kashi Vishvanath Temple on the Ganges at Varanasi. Varanasi is the city known to devout Hindus as Kashi, which means "salvation." The devout Hindu believes that if one dies in Varanasi, her soul will be free from ever again incarnating to live this painful life again. So far, for me, this has been true, although my life above, in the temple, was a mere century ago, ten years after the Indian people won their nation's independence.

The sea-faerie life is magical and good. But I enjoyed living above, as well. Life in the temple, in Kashi, was peaceful, with many colorful gods wearing garlands of marigolds to watch over me. I loved wading in the peaceful waters of the beautiful River Ganges. The temple gardens were lush, and the people who came to worship were gentle. The monkeys and the mice were like pesky children, constantly clamoring for attention, but what entertaining pests they were!

Today is a lovely, turquoise day, when the sand on the ocean floor is calm. All is light, and lovely. Looking up is reminiscent of the days when we looked up and saw sky, in Lemuria. The air was clean and clear, and greens were rich, as they are today. Sea roses are blooming, as they did in Lemuria; they are as large as giant clams, and bright orange and pink. Rona, our queen and mother, seems carefree today, and laughs like a child, at nothing and everything. Her laughter sounds like the music of water splashing on rocks, or sometimes it is like a spoon tapping very gently on a crystal goblet. Laughter dresses her. It folds around her, and you can see the colors of her laughter when she walks. She laughs in bright fuchsia and golden orange, and these colors swirl sharply all around her body. But what pleases her most is when she hears me laugh. Then the warmth of her sunny love radiates, and rushes all over me. She is not the normal, self-centered Queen, our beloved Rona. And I know the source of her joy today: the woman football player in the world above, Pepper McCullah, pleases her to no end. I am very jealous of this Pepper, and feel myself wanting to make jealous mischief.

This Pepper has written my beloved queen a letter, in answer to a letter Rona wrote to her. Queen Rona never told me she wrote to this woman football player. A football player, indeed! (I would've given the fan-feathered brow to one of her brothers, but Rona insisted it was Pepper who would wear it.) How dare this Pepper write so intimately to our royal Queen? Her letter is interminable; she goes on and on in that dreadful, modern, American language of hers. Does she imagine our Queen has nothing better to do than chat with a football player? What is it about this young woman my queen finds so lovable? I do not care for this Pepper, and am dismayed with myself. I am an Ascended Master, supposedly removed from ancient, petty emotions such as jealousy. Rona would say there is a lesson here for me, and I will meditate on what it might be.

From the Earth Memories Archives
Compiled by Pepper McCullah,
Clan of the Fan-Feathered Brow
Earth Year 2030

My introduction to life as a Wisdom Retriever and Sun Quartz Field Warrior began with a brief note from "Queen Rona" that my mother had given me. Her letter had basically introduced herself to me, and told me I'd been chosen as a Wisdom Retriever. (In the letter, I was instructed never to repeat its contents, and to this, I remain true.) This was my lengthy response to her note:

Dear Queen Rona,

What are you Queen of? I can't find your country, Koba, anywhere in the *World Atlas*. Anyway, your letter to me was so strange and fascinating. Oddly, I feel I've always known you. I feel comfortable telling you everything. I will keep your letter's contents secret. Honestly, I think people would think it's a prank, anyway! Imagine me getting a letter about my important duty, and this journey I'm supposed to go on! But I'm going to catch the ball and run with it, and spill my heart out to you.

It is so great to get back to the typewriter; gone are the days, as you know, when my people could just go to our computers to write. Computer time has been rationed since I was ten, because of the energy demands on a limited number of fuel cells. We can't seem to produce them fast enough! But this solar-powered typewriter is similar to what some great literary heroes wrote on, centuries ago, and it makes a comforting clackety-clack noise I like.

I have this gigantic letter in me I have to write. I'm feeling perky these days. I am grateful, so grateful, for everything, and, considering all that has happened to me, I know everyone would find it unbelievable. My world rocks!

Such a short time ago, when I'd won the MVP Trophy in the 2029 Oceanbowl game, I felt pretty pleased with myself, but it wasn't quite like this. This is right up there with meeting Marion Jones, my Idol, who turned fifty just before I signed with the 49-er's.

How funny it was in the beginning, when all anybody cared about was what happened in the locker room. It was a national obsession! All these red-faced, angry men and women worrying about how the woman football player would take a shower. It was so nothing; the guys were happy to stay outside and give me first shower, and total privacy. Nobody cared. I mean, most of Earth had been destroyed! So little matters anymore, after that.

Queen Rona, I love football. Always have. Love of the football started racing through my blood when I was a scrawny little girl, born between two jock brothers. Growing up in the Earth Core tunnels, while billions of people died above us, we prayed, we learned, and we played football. Wide receiver is the only position I ever played, and it's all I ever wanted to play. All the guys on the block were all big and old and hairy. I was eight when I started to show potential. My brother Collin would go over the play, and say, "Pepper, get open, and catch the ball, or I'll pound you." I always got open, somehow, and I always, always caught it.

Poor Mom was always trying to get me inside: wisdom meditations, piano lessons, ballet, (that I should've done, a la Joe Namath, almost a century ago—it would've been good for my game). It never worked. I loved playing football. After the Re-Emergence, and everybody lived above ground again, I dusted all the guys in Pop Warner. Mine was such a great, small town, by the time I got to high school, everybody was cool with me. I was the football hero of Zephyr Cove in high school, and won them their first trophy since The Great Emergence and Rebuilding. In those days, I was a little blurb on the bottoms of pages in _Time_ and _People_. _Sports Illustrated for Kids_ did the first full-length feature on me, where I first stated, "I intend to play for the National Football League." A few more phones started ringing.

Naturally, everyone noticed I'm cute, but I don't look as good in clothes as the girly girls. I feel beautiful, Queen Rona. I love my pretty face with the feathery eyebrows, my way-pumped arms, and all my hard—won muscles and bruises.

I chose to attend Stanford for so many reasons. First, of course, my parents, famous scientists, went there. If they hadn't studied the changing orbits of the Amor Asteroids, we'd be part of the ocean floor, with the rest of California's coast. Besides, Stanford is so pro-women athletes. I knew they wouldn't mess with my dreams, and I was right. Stanford is full of brainy people who are entirely full of themselves and their brilliance. I always kept looking over my shoulder, positive someone would say, "Excuse me, but we've made a terrible mistake. You're really not as smart as the rest of us, and you'll have to leave." But they didn't; I worked hard, and did well. The cool thing is, if you are one of them, Stanford people will fight to the death for you and your rights. So I did the Cardinals thing, and I was really, really good. Yes, I was a woman, but so what? I caught the friggin' ball, we beat UCP in the OceanBowl, and who cares if I used some Placerville family's garden hose to shower with all my clothes on? (By the time the news media quit interviewing me, all the guys were in the shower.) I was too happy to care! I just told my brothers to hit me with the garden hose.

Most bright college kids wanted to major in World Mythology after surviving the near destruction of Earth that began on December 23, 2012, exactly as the Mayans had predicted. I majored in World Mythology because I felt I would find an ancient piece of myself there. I remember the gorgeous, brilliant professor who made me weep when he said, "We have always studied mythology and literature to learn compassion toward men and women, but now, having lost six billion people, and half the land mass on this earth, we study to learn compassion for Mother Earth, as well." I was already a student of compassion; I hungered to study it in a world where people had killed each other over oil and megawatts. I needed to understand a world where humanity, Earth, and even the heavens rage with violence. Violence is part of life itself.

Mind you, I still haven't perfected compassion. Compassion for ordinary people means you never get hissy with those who fumble. You forgive everyone, saying, "We're all doing the very best we can do with what we have to work with." Although things haven't worked out according to anyone's original plans, I am glad about both the compassion and my love of words and myth. When you're on your butt as much as I am these days, books are cherished friends.

I sweep away the pity ferociously, first thing, when I meet someone new. Like with Frank, my physical therapist. What a nice man he is! It started with his nervousness at meeting me. I thought it was a pity thing, and I wanted to get chilly, but saw honest admiration in his eyes. He wanted me to sign an autograph for his niece. A bit more than my P.T., he is becoming a friend. He's a great sports man; he knows football, like, dating back to the early twentieth century.

Queen Rona, every strange thing that happens in our lives happens for a reason, and maybe I haven't completely figured out my place in the scheme of things. But I know that the day of my accident, my life was transformed, and I was filled with a Light that has never dimmed.

It was a good hit. Nothing dirty about it. I just flew too high in the air, jack-knifed, and came down wrong. I was out for a few minutes, but when I came to, the greatest, most profoundly spiritual experience of my life transformed me. I felt thousands of peoples' active love for me. Every single person in Placerville Ocean Park was sending me love in this holy, blessed moment. I heard their silent prayers, and tasted the salt in the tears on their cheeks as they prayed.

"Please get up, Pepper," their lips mouthed, and their love filled me with this incredible light. I already knew I would never walk again, but the joy and beauty of all that love was infinitely more powerful than anything before or since. People are good, Queen Rona. We screw up, we fumble, but in our hearts, there is so much love and goodness.

I'm thrilled I got to play football for the NFL, but that's not why I was put on this earth. My real job begins now, and it's one I lovingly embrace. I feel honored to have been chosen for such an important job, and I am more than a little intimidated. Mind you, a 150-pound woman who has faced 250-pound tackles knows a great deal about intimidation. Speed is what keeps you alive, and speed is what I need now. There isn't too much time, according to you.

And so, my dear Queen, I end this interminably long letter imploring you for direction. I'm a jock. I've got this awesome, four-wheel mountain bike, and I'm starting to win competitions in down-hill racing. I love PP skiing. Am I really up to this job you and the others have chosen me to perform? I'm no New Earth Master, you know. My mom tried her hardest to teach me the wisdom of our ancient clan, and I got pretty good at the ibis flame ritual thing. But my technique needs a lot of work. Help me, please.

All My Love and Light, Pepper McCullah

After this first letter that I experienced the magic of Koba for the first time. I set the letter on my bedside table, then watched in won-der as it floated out the window and evaporated. Then, a beautiful, new letter, wrapped in blue ribbons, sat on the bedside table where I'd placed mine to Queen Rona. It was from Queen Rona, herself.

Dear Pepper,

You are so full of light! It is no wonder to me that you were chosen as the one to carry the fan-feathered brow beyond this realm into the next. I am glad you are the chosen one. I am glad a soul with such a joyful, physical Earth body was chosen.

Our spirits were put inside fleshy bodies for a reason, and the rea-son is Joy. To feel the wind on your face, and the sun on your shoulders, is a great, blissful wonder. To see high mountains covered with snow, and waves crashing against the shore—to feel the power of these manifestations of the Great Creation deep inside your soul—fills you with overflowing Joy. You have great capacity for Joy in the physical realm, and that empowers the Greatest Souls. Spirituality blossoms from natural, earthly living; it is not separate. It is from earthly living that the bouquet of spiritual life blossoms forth. Never forget that.

Your football joys will live on in your heart forever. Watching you play football was enthralling. You'd lift your strong arms gracefully to reach and catch the ball nearly every time. You then ran with everything inside you. Your running was raw poetry: those magnificent, strong thighs pushing you impossibly ever forward, while you hugged the ball like a ferocious mother bear cub would hold her baby against danger. I loved your cuts; you faked the big men every time. Your movements were balletic. You leaped and twirled in a Martha Graham-inspired dance, and it was rare for anyone to catch you, once you had the ball.

I understand you're skiing, now, in that sit-down contraption, and doing some downhill racing on a four-wheel bike. I confess, I worry. Much is resting on those beautiful, strong shoulders of yours!

Continue to explore your beautiful spirit and heart, my beloved Pepper. I am never far, and I love this "letter-writing thing," as you would call it. Indeed, as I read through this letter, I see have picked up a great deal of your manner of modern American expression!

You will soon journey into the next phase of your travels. You will make many long journeys, into incredible, distant realms. Ascended Masters through the millennia have referred to it as "The Arduous Journey Toward Self." Hopefully, these experiences—far different from your experiences in this lifetime—will never "creep you out," to use your words. The souls you will meet are, for the most part, gentle. The Startling Ones, as I refer to the Spirits from the Dark Side, should not frighten one who has faced 200-pound cornerbacks. If you do feel terribly afraid, always reach for me in your heart. I will be there in an instant. Think of me as one of those coaches with the headset linked to the headset inside your helmet.

Pepper, go forward, always knowing you are loved by so many hundreds of thousands. Let that love always light your way, for that is your power. I love you so much!

Love and Light,

Queen Rona

A SEA FAERIE'S TORMENT

From the Earth Memories Archives
Compiled by Marla, Sea Faerie
Keeper of Memories

I am a jealous Marla today, reading the letter my Queen sent this Pepper. I feel myself wishing to cause mischief, and it is a delicious feeling I have not experienced in thousands of years. I must find some naughty, mischievous way for Pepper to displease Queen Rona. I will think of a plan to make her look less radiant, and myself a little moreso.

Forget Pepper! I must return to work! As Sea Faerie Keeper of Memories, I must make sense of human history, and the history of the Clan of the Fan-Feathered Brow, down through the Millennia. Because of their destiny as race-savers, the Clan of the Fan-Feathered Brow must be studied within the context of their human history.

Their history is incredibly calamitous. Their twenty-first century alone began with Greed King maneuvers for ultimate power. That ghastly money they hunger for turns them into madly chaotic forces of evil. They use religion to control their people in their mad quests, but love of God has nothing to do with this evil. Divisiveness has nothing to do with God.

In the twentieth century came the growing need for energy to fuel what they believed was an advanced technology. (All humans, in every developing civilization, are convinced they are extremely advanced!) Theirs was a civilization based entirely in the material realm. They imagined their funny, busy brains alone contained the answers to all existence. Imagine, brains without heart or spirit. It's a wonder this civilization lasted as long as it did! Their destruction in 2012 was inexorable, for they'd forgotten their history of heart and spirit.

Their scientists and astronomers discovered, even before the end of the twentieth century, 6,000 Amor Asteroids that could potentially cross the earth's orbit. One in particular, they feared, was wobbling in its orbit, and could easily enter Earth's atmosphere and cause unparalleled destruction. In the first month of 2002, in fact, a very large meteor the size of several of Pepper's football fields crashed into the Indian Ocean.

Scientists alerted their governments, but governments worldwide were busy warring with insidious terrorists who blew up cities without warning. Terrible war raged all over the world: a war that poisoned the air with disease and the ground with destruction. It was a war waged on earth, in the skies above her, and in cyberspace.

The ancient Hopi—descendants of my own brothers and sisters—had long ago skipped across the seven Pacific islands of Mu as they were exploding. They came to America, and they knew exactly what would happen to their new homeland. They'd seen it before, in their own Motherland. The Hopi, whose name means "Peaceful Ones," said their Mother Earth would again respond to all this destruction of her air, her water, her soil, and her people's hearts. They urged Earth people to remember their history. The Hopi joined hands and walked for miles across the battlefields, trying to stop the destruction. They predicted that if humans did not stop their battles for power on Earth, the purification would come hard and swift, as prophesied for so many millennia.

The fortunate few who did listen to the astronomers and the Hopi began tunneling early. Brilliant scientists—from the world's foremost universities—including Jim and Alaiya McCullah (Pepper's parents), astronomers from Stanford University—built sophisticated underground dwellings near the earth's core, and stored enough food to last four years. They built gardens, with artificial light powered by hydrogen fuel cells, deep beneath the earth. They built forests. Knowing a massive cataclysm would wipe out Earth's plant and animal life, scientists took as much of that life as Earth's womb could hold, below. They created an intricate power system that ran efficiently on hydrogen fuel cells. Pulling the hydrogen from the abundant methane gas from their animal and plant waste gave them all the power they would need. They took their most precious books, stockpiles of food, and animals they wished to keep from extinction. Finally, they took their families and friends below the surface in 2010, when Pepper McCullah was two years old.

Then, in 2012—just as the ancient Mayans and modern Hopi had predicted—violence rained from the heavens. The massive comet, later named "Gonaquadet" after the Tlingit Indians' terrible sea monster, surged into earth's atmosphere on December 23rd, at the speed of Earth people's 33,000 miles per hour. Energy equivalent to a one billion megaton nuclear bomb was released, blowing away Earth's atmosphere. When the comet—six miles in diameter—hit the floor of the Indian Ocean, we sea faeries watched helplessly as it only half submerged before it vaporized.

Tidal waves, thousands of miles high, raged instantly, drowning entire continents, just as my own Mu had once drowned. Earth's wealthiest and poorest nations were submerged together in a mercifully swift tower of mighty ocean. My beloved India is no more, and the sands of Arabia now mingle with the sands at the bottom of the sea. Although Africa and Southern Asia were hardest hit, no continent was left untouched. Island countries were swallowed by the thousand foot high waves, and earthquakes savagely ripped continents apart.

A catastrophe of this magnitude had only been seen sixty-five million years before, when a similar-sized comet wiped out the dinosaurs, and changed all life on earth thereafter. Just as in that time of violent change, weeks and weeks passed before the winds and tidal waves subsided. The blast's energy caused nitrogen and oxygen to mix, and the acid rains that followed killed what little had been left. Forest fires generated from the heat of the comet's impact raged unchecked for months, all over Earth. Hundreds of miles of ash from the fires filled the atmosphere, and left the planet dark.

For two years, the Earth was black as night. The sun's light and warmth were blotted out completely by the miles of ash in the atmosphere. Temperatures dropped, and plants on land and in the sea died. (Ascended Masters living below the sea had guided the ocean-dwelling species to another dimension, because Earth without dolphins' laughter was unacceptable. Details of this exodus of the ocean-dwelling ones follow later, as this was my "pet project," to use an Earth expression.)

Small, surviving colonies all over the world continued to live below, in their Earth Core tunnel palaces, until The Great Emergence in 2014. The people of Earth learned to live together in artificial, small spaces. They learned ancient ways of harmony and peace, and the unity of body-mind-spirit; they re-learned some of the ancient ways of mind over matter, lost down through the millennia during the Civilizations of Materialism.

Scientists had planted monitors above ground during the years below, ever-measuring the light and toxic conditions. They promised their tunnel dwellers they would emerge one day, and build a new life of unparalleled peace and harmony.

There was, finally, a day in May, when the monitors proclaimed that life could again be supported on Earth. Gingerly, a few of the bravest souls ventured into the hazy light. What they saw made them weep: an Earth that looked more like a barren moon.

The human spirit is magnificent in its way, however. One bright-eyed, indomitable man saw a green, living leaf and rejoiced. This science engineer, Jim McCullah, rejoiced in the sun's hazy, feeble light.

He wept and knelt to kiss the leaf. He rejoiced again when he noticed, in the hollowed-out shadow of a building, a growing sprout of a houseplant. Perched saucily on this one small leaf was a lady-bug—a brazen tribute to the miracle of life. Jim named the ladybug Phoenix, after the lone, legendary Egyptian bird who rose from the ashes after consuming herself in flames. She symbolized the hope of resurrection: life reborn.

The digging out began. Seeing an Earth that had once been so blue and green and warm reduced to barren, bleak, cold rubble broke many hearts. The Earth Core Tunnel Palace Dwellers were so glad to be above, in the sunlight, however, they ventured forth with firm resolve. They carried their determination to build a world of peace and beauty, and wore it like a glowing badge. Walking in peace, they loved their battered Earth.

The Earth Core Tunnel Palace Dwellers met quickly the New Earth People, and were overjoyed to find survivors who'd somehow managed to survive above after the cataclysm. The New Earth People were fierce and resourceful; they'd survived by raiding grocery stores, and by harnessing the ferocious, howling winds and waters to supply them with much-needed heat. They eyed the Earth Core Tunnel Palace Dwellers suspiciously at first, for their supplies grew scarcer every day, and every new face represented a threat to their survival. Their lives had been lived in a far more harsh, elemental way than the Earth Core Tunnel Dwellers, and the two cultures clashed.

The Earth Core Tunnel Palace Dwellers from the western region of America picked Alaiya McCullah, Pepper's mother, as their Ambassador. An olive-skinned, beautiful mother of three who radiated gentleness and compassion, she had eyebrows shaped like feather fans above her lush, green eyes. She had studied the Ancient Ways during the time she'd lived below, in the very womb of her mother, Earth, and she was the spiritual leader for the Earth Core Tunnel Palace Dwellers.

Alaiya went to the leader of the western region of America's New Earth People—a man named Jason Lawrence. Jason had once been a famous film star. Still handsome, despite the years' struggles, he was dynamic. His people had chosen him for these qualities, as well as for his resourceful creativity in procuring power, warmth, and food for other survivors. He was also good at rallying sagging spirits in the ways of the old Hollywood: he'd gathered other entertainers, and they'd sing and dance.

Jason did not rebuff Alaiya's motherly embrace. They wept together, and forged a bond with their tears. Alaiya took him below, to the Earth Core Tunnel Palaces, and showed him sights he hadn't seen in years: green trees growing tall, and living animals the New Earth people had assumed were now completely extinct. Jason understood the impact their unity would have on the planet: with the Earth Core Tunnel Palace Dwellers' living plants and animals, and the New Earth People's resourceful new way of living harmoniously on the earth as it now was, they could become one race, better than ever.

A bitter-hearted man stood beside Jason, however, scornfully observing the bond growing between the Earth Core Tunnel people and the New Earth people. His name was Tronot, and his dark lineage traced all the way back to the evil Memsek in ancient Egypt. Tronot, immersed in survival during the terrible years above that had followed Gonaquadet, had vowed he would someday possess complete power over the very heavens that had rained down such suffering.

For now, however, Tronot's bitterness went unnoticed. The planned uniting of Earth Core Tunnel dwellers and New Earth citizens was a glorious plan. All Kobans celebrated beneath the sea. Alas, other Greed Kings besides Tronot had survived the cataclysm, living the harsh life above in its aftermath. Apparently, the ways of war and power struggles were habits they could not break.

Civilization as the people had known it before the cataclysm was almost, but not completely destroyed. The old life could never return, but gradually, with the return of sunlight, the people's fondness for "the good ole' days" led them to re-create the things they remembered loving. Humanity rethought their civilization before they rebuilt it. They kept the things they had loved well—for example, football and hockey remained—but they tried to do away with some of the things they hadn't loved, such as greed and squabbling. From 2014-2020 were the Rebuilding years. Universities reopened, with all students spending part of their day with hammers and nails, building their campuses.

In the 2012 "Great Purification," as the Hopi refer to the cataclysm, no continent was spared, but some survived fairly intact. North America lost all of her western coast and all of her eastern and southern shores for hundreds of miles, but much of her vast inland remains. Worldwide, over six billion lives were lost. (I understand that families are now encouraged to have many children in places where, before the cataclysm, it was a crime to bear more than one child.) Much of the land once known as the Yucatan, in Mexico, is now beneath the sea. Chunks of my Motherland once lay bleaching in the Yucatan sun for millennia, but now, Mu's remains lie beneath the sea as well. It pleases me to swim here and gather these beautiful, ancient stones from my Motherland.

The one glory emerging from the catastrophe, and perhaps the answer to human survival, lay in the sad destruction of the Egyptian Sphinx. I am grateful I knew well that mystical creature, before it crumbled into Egyptian sands! But when the Sphinx crumbled, the Hall of Records, buried for six millennia, was finally unearthed. (The bones of Nanu were also unearthed, but I get ahead in my telling.)

While the peoples of Earth spent their last drops of fossil fuel, and while they argued over where to bury their toxic nuclear waste, answers to their energy problems lay in the unearthed rubble in what was left of the Egyptian desert.

The Energy Agenda followed: whatever land remained above or below sea was excavated, in search of the small, remaining reserves of fossil fuel. The last barrel of fossil fuel was spent in 2018. Rockets with infrared searching mechanisms soared in vain above spots of Earth thought to possess any reserves of oil. The era of the polluting combustible engine was dead forever. The Earth Core Tunnels' clean, efficient fuel cells could not, and have not, at this writing, been produced as fast as the growing need for them. (If all goes well in the Sun Quartz Fields, of course, they, too, will soon be obsolete.)

Finally, in 2020, the world settled down to face the realization their fossil fuel was gone, and that fuel cells, supplied externally by hydrogen, would power their new world of non-combustible machines. Earth began to show renewed vigor in her cleansed waters and skies.

One very brave Wisdom Keeper from the Clan of the Frozen Fields, Lars Grenden (father of Todd Grenden, Pepper's ice hockey friend whom these records will soon introduce), risked his life to poke around the ruins of the Hall of Records in Egypt. Lo, he discovered acres and acres of Wisdom Texts from Mu and Atlantis. Among these texts lay the Secrets of the Sun Quartz Fields, written hastily, some thirteen thousand years earlier, before the Land of Mu exploded.

I share this brief history only as a bit of background for readers in another century, who now study the lifting of our veil. There is so much to tell! As I write the events of Earth's year 2030, wind, sun, water, and hydrogen fuel cells are used to fuel the new technology's hungry flames. Despite constant, rolling "energy blackouts," and "brown-outs," as humans refer to them, life has settled somewhat.

The texts from Atlantis and Mu that our fan-feathered Nanu died to protect (that story will be told, I promise!) have been stored in the Wisdom Palace. Hopefully, some of the old civilizations of materialism can meld with the far more ancient civilizations of mind, heart, and spirit over matter. If humanity can live in both the material realm and the realm of spirit, mind, and heart, they will survive, in perfect peace and harmony. Their leaders, at last, know this.

The Wisdom Palace is built of rose quartz that rests majestically in the Sierra Mountains above sapphire blue Lake Tahoe. I confess enjoyment of my assignment inscribing the tales of Pepper and the Wisdom Palace, because I love watching sun diamonds scatter across the sapphire blue, sacred waters of Lake Tahoe. I believe the gods spared this mountain lake in the 2012 cataclysm because of the great pleasure from enjoying its beauty. I feel the holiness of the place. It is a grand place for a Sea Faerie to light!

My glowing, golden antennae now alert me to something terrible happening above. Alaiya is performing the Ibis Ritual. I watch: as in ancient days, from the time of the Pharoahs, Alaiya—descendant of Nanu—smooths the dirt on the shore of the swampy bird sanctuary near Lake Tahoe. Drawing with her finger, she makes the ancient Egyptian symbols which spell the name of the Great Mother Ibis. She is in a trance as she tosses dried reeds upon the name written in the soil. A flame jumps from the reeds, and Caleina and the Mother Ibis appear before her. Alaiya levitates slightly from the ground.

"I want to know what Pepper faces," Alaiya says. "Tronot blinded the Wisdom Keeper Ulena by throwing acid into her eyes. I am afraid for my daughter!"

Caleina and the Mother Ibis look at Alaiya sadly, and flap their wings. A vision appears before Alaiya. A battle rages in space. Tronot is wielding a huge gun. Alaiya loses her concentration, falls to the ground, and weeps beside the fire's smoking embers. Caleina and Mother Ibis spread their wings about Alaiya gently before they vanish.

ASSESSING THE JOURNEY

From the Earth Memories Archives
Compiled by Pepper McCullah
Clan of the Fan-Feathered Brow
Earth Year 2030

Mom asked me, "Dear, about this letter from Queen Rona. Do you know exactly who she is, and how important she is?"

"I'm not completely sure, Mom. She wrote me this strange letter, and as soon as I read it, I felt I'd known her forever. I feel our family has always known her. She feels like a relative, and when I write to her, I feel I am approaching my destiny and reaching back into my ancient past at the same time, if that makes any sense."

Mom flipped her long, chestnut hair behind her. She looked worried behind her beautiful, green eyes, but she sat beside me and kissed my forehead. "It makes complete sense, Pepper. You will soon understand all that I have been trying to teach you, since you were tiny, about our Clan of the Fan-Feathered Brow."

"Hey, Mom, look! My quarterbackie, Bruce-the-Deuce, made the front page of the paper! I've got to write him."

Dear Bruce,

It was great to see you on the front page. I'm glad to hear all the guys are praying for me, and gladder still you won the last game for me. 35-28 was a little close, though. Bruce, you had an awesome game; what an incredible pass you threw for that final touchdown in the last ten seconds! I'm flattered it was for me.

I'm doing well, honest. What if God had said, before any of this happened, "Pepper, you have two choices: you can be the first woman ever to play in the NFL and win the MVP in an OceanBowl, with the little downer glitch that you'll get paralyzed early in the following season, OR, you can skip the whole football thing, and never be paralyzed." Do you think I would've given up one thing I've experienced? I don't think so.

"The worst thing about being paralyzed is my dad's suffering. For Mom, all that matters is I'm alive. Mom, however, is not like other people. She loves who I am inside, and who I am inside is no different if my legs don't work right. Mom also says it was my injury that gave me the key to my own destiny, whatever that means!

Dad was my football buddy. He loved me, of course, but he especially loved what I did. For Dad, I was what I did. Maybe he feels guilty, too, because I inherited his love of a football. When I was tiny, in the Earth Core Tunnels, before I could really catch, Dad and I would sit on the floor and sniff the football. Think of it, Bruce. I loved the smell of pigskin before I could even catch! But do you think I would have changed one thing about my life with Dad? We had a blast together, and love of the game ran in our blood, pulsing at the same beat. Heck, you know, I can still catch the ball; maybe he and I will someday play together again.

Listen, if you get a chance, can you please assure people I did NOT get hurt because I'm a woman? You cannot imagine how much that irritates me. I'm attending sessions of this Gimpy Athletes consciousness-raising support group—please don't tell anyone I call it that—and there are a whole bunch of gorgeous male athletes who are in wheelchairs. Bad luck is not gender specific, believe me.

Hey, there is a guy in this wheelchair group I like, and if this gets to the media, I'll grind your butt into the street with my wheelchair. I'm flirting with Todd Grenden, the MVP hockey player, big time. He is one good-looking guy. There is a dark, sad place in him, similar to mine. He doesn't want it to be there. I mean, he tries to be his cheer-leader-self all the time, but it's killing him that he can't play hockey anymore.

I look forward to the sessions with these beat-up athletes, because these are the only people who know EXACTLY how I feel, and how much I hate being in a wheelchair. I've only gone a couple times, but I feel it's going to take me somewhere powerful. We meditate, which is very peaceful, and the leader of the group is this magical blind woman, Ulena. She takes us into our spirit—the soul—where we are without limitation. I like it!

Anyway, women should not be afraid to follow their football dreams because I got hurt. That's absurd. Every dream has its risks and its dangers. When I get a new dream, I'll tell you about it, but I'm sure you know it will involve danger and risk. I'm a dangerous dreamer!

I love you, Bruce, but tell the other guys not to be jealous, because I love all of them, too. (Spotty's gross card made me laugh so hard! He's such a punk!)

Love 'ya, Pepper

THE JOURNEYS BEGIN

From the Earth Memories Archives
Compiled by Pepper McCullah
Clan of the Fan-Feathered Brow
Earth Year 2030

I was invited to the Wisdom Palace, which has a golden-domed hall for injured athletes. Honestly, I think I accepted the invitation mostly to get away from my depressed dad and two brothers. I could not stand the weight of their suffering bearing down on my already-burdened shoulders. They wanted to "fix" me, wave a wand and make me stand up and run. They are torn-up people—as if I'm not! I had to get away. I had to go someplace where I could say, "this SUCKS, being in a wheelchair," without making anyone more depressed than they already are by my new, handicapped status. It's crazy to think I don't miss running free, and I should be able to say it, once in awhile, without breaking someone's heart.

A woman with the most mellifluous voice, Ulena, called on the phone to invite me to the Wisdom Palace. It was so wonderful talking to Ulena, I did not want to hang up.

These tiny lessons, and my subsequent readings, were only the beginnings of my strange, new life. It is odd to write of the journeys I began taking, because I am not the "Spiritual Journeys" type of person. I am a Jock: a lover of pretzels and football and guys!

Yes, I'm a well-read jock, and, besides sports writers, my favorite writers are women: Virginia Woolf, Jane Austen, Anne Rice, Isabel Allende, Alice Walker, Toni Morrison, Amy Tan, and Barbara King-solver. They are all Women Passion Writers. If it is my new purpose in life to write about all that is happening, and is about to happen, I don't understand why I didn't get any of my hero women writers' eloquence.

To continue with my love of earthly pleasures: I love obnoxious rock music, sung by people with painted skulls. (Since their time on electric instruments is limited, I have to say I love all the acoustical instruments everyone's invented, lately.) I love chocolate, and deep-fried anything, and I fidget if I sit in a building too long. I am, in short, the quintessential Earth Woman!

I have always loved God with my whole heart, but I have never been a Holy Roller, or a meditative, New Earth type. I respect the New Earth people, who make their own power, and who've invented all sorts of machines that run without electricity; they've created a non-invasive way to live with our limited resources. They know the ancient, mystical ways of Atlantis and Mu. But I am not one of them. I have this new friend I write to, Queen Rona, who says the spiritual life blossoms from the earthy life, and that makes me feel better about just being me.

This is all very difficult for me, and it will be hard for me to write down properly, but I believe—no, I know—all this has happened to me for some distinct purpose. With all that I have, and all that I am, in my own, not-fabulous style, I must write everything that has hap-pened, and be true to it all.

After Ulena invited me to the Wisdom Palace, the President of the United States called! What a thrill for my folks, to have the Chief-ette herself call!

"Pepper McCullah? I am so glad to talk to you, although I must first scold you for the mural of 'Marla, the Sea Faerie' you did on the side of the White House. What were you thinking?"

"What?" Had the Chieffette gone mad? I swear the sound like a tiny tinkle of laughter filled the air around me, as I tried to sputter a protest. I would never do such a weird thing. "Ms. President, I can't even draw! Who is this Marla, and why would anyone sign my name to a mural of her? I'm in a wheelchair, remember? How could I possibly get up high enough to paint on the White House?"

"Oh, don't worry about it. The mural was very cute. We painted over it before the media ever got wind of it." She offered some brief condolences because of my injury, and she told me she'd been a longtime fan of my magic with the football. Then she told me what an incredible honor it was that I'd been invited to become a Wisdom Retriever. That, she said, had always been her biggest dream, but she was rejected, so she had to settle for being a President. I was psyched! I'm off to become a Wisdom Retriever, whatever the heck that is!

INSIDE THE WISDOM PALACE

From the Earth Memories Archives
Compiled by Pepper McCullah
Clan of the Fan-Feathered Brow
Earth Year 2030

The Wisdom Palace was built in 2020, a full decade ago, after all the smoke had cleared from Gonaquadet's mass destruction. The magnificent temple was made completely of rose quartz at my mother's suggestion. Its spires make it look like a Gothic cathedral. Since it is of rose quartz, I can faintly see through the building. As my mother wheeled me toward the huge, gorgeous palace, she told me how proud she was of me. I barely heard, I was so amazed by the palace.

Perched on a hanging cliff, the Wisdom Palace stands alone with an all-encompassing view of snow-covered Mt. Tallac and Lake Tahoe. Apparently, after Gonaquadet's worldwide cataclysm of 2012, Tahoe was found to be the safest place on earth. The Ancient Wisdom Teachers say that before Gonaquadet, Lake Tahoe experienced tiny earthquakes almost daily, and that was because people there remembered their history. The ley lines never clogged. (That's why my parents had chosen the area for the Earth Core Tunnels their team built.) Interestingly, the slight faults in the plates below the lake had fused together in the shaking of Gonaquadet's cataclysmic aftermath. On the entire planet, this beautiful land was deemed the safest from being shredded.

All sorts of holy temples sprang up here after that, but I'm glad the TRPA—the local power behind building, up here—stayed tough about not letting the population increase too much. I had been born here, before my parents went underground, and my father and mother were invited to return here because they are two of the most prominent scientists of our time. My mother, Alaiya, respected as a spiritual advisor, has devoted her life to learning the wisdom of the ancient past, in hopes of finding a peaceful, balanced way to live with our Mother, the Earth.

The Wisdom Palace houses the ancient texts from Atlantis and Mu, which were finally unearthed from the Hall of Records, hidden beneath the Egyptian Sphinx's rear paws for 13,000 years. In 2014, two years after Gonaquadet, much of Egypt and the Sphinx imploded into the sand, and the ancient Hall of Records was uncovered by Todd Grenden's dad, Lars. Discovery of these texts, had, of course, changed the entire world's idea of itself. History books had all been proven wrong, and, along with all the other rebuilding of our planet, we had to rewrite our entire history. Digging out had consumed the people of Earth for the next six years, until everything finally settled down, about 2020.

My mom now wheeled me into the Wisdom Palace's Golden Domed Athlete's Hall, where seventeen other injured athletes fidgeted nervously in their wheelchairs. I was the last to arrive, and Mom bent over me with tears in her eyes.

"You are very brave, my darling. I love you so much."

"Me, too, Mom." Everyone was staring. I kissed her, and she turned and waved at me, as if to see me this way for the last time.

Todd Grenden, the ice hockey phenomenon—the MVP for the 2029 Stanley Cup Championship Game—sat near me. He was the masterful Center for the Ottawa Senators, until a terrible plane crash left him paralyzed. He'd parachuted from way too high, and his back broke from the force of landing on his feet; still, he was mighty lucky to be alive.

I smiled at him. Such a really handsome man! He had a mess of curly, dark blonde hair, and big blue eyes. He smiled back, and if you know anything about hockey, you know how amazed I was when I saw he had all his teeth!

I could have sat there swooning, looking at this gorgeous hockey player all day, but a tall, beautiful woman with strange, Alaskan Husky-whitish-blue eyes started to speak. I quickly realized she was blind by the way she sort of looked at us, but sort of did not look at us.

"My name is Ulena, and I welcome all of you to the Wisdom Palace. We are in a time of crisis, and you have all been chosen as Earth's great healers. You are the greatest warriors our people have, and the earth is asking you for the ultimate sacrifice.

"The final battle with the Greed Kings is about to take place. Lands and peoples who retired from involvement with Earth affairs 13,000 years ago are rising up to join us in this battle. If we lose, and the Greed Kings win, here is what our planet will look like in a mere one hundred years:"

Using only her closed eyes, Ulena projected a vast, 3-D image on the domed ceiling above us. The picture was ugly, one of a choked, stinking, ruined Earth suddenly swallowed by an enormous mushroom cloud. Suddenly, in this telepathic "film," earth exploded into bits that flew into the universe.

Ulena continued. "Koba, the Underwater World, is rising up, joining us for the first time in thousands of years, to fight this battle. Mind you, they are not entirely the same kind of humans as we are. They are Ascended Masters who have spent the last thirteen thousand years evolving so they can live underwater.

"Koba, the Underwater World?" Todd asked. His big eyes rounded into o-shaped pools of astonished blue.

"Oh, yes. Vestiges of learning from Lemuria—the Land of Mu—which sank about 13,000 years ago, are still alive in Tibet, but the wisest and most powerful of the Lemurians established the Underwater World of Koba, beneath the sea in the River of Life."

No wonder I couldn't find her on any maps!

"Rona is Queen of Koba, and you will all meet her at some point. Kanta, her husband, is the mightiest of Kings. One of the good things to come out of the radioactive poisoning of the seas is the scope of Kanta's incredible powers when he comes above. To cleanse his beloved seas of toxins, he took them all unto himself. He well might have died, but instead, because of his massive love and self-sacrifice, his powers are limitless. The poisons, mixed with his love of the seas and their creatures, only made him stronger. He is a great, legendary warrior, but a little on the crabby side, so don't irritate him if you can help it.

"When Atlantis exploded, 10,000 years ago, her peoples spread out all over the planet. Vestiges of Atlantean culture are still alive everywhere today, especially in the Sioux and Apache Nations, but the wisest ones from Atlantis joined the Lemurian Mentors in Koba, under the sea. It is a lucious, peaceful world. I have visited often, but the cycle is changing, and it is again time for the wise ones beneath to return to the surface, and reclaim Earth for the Greater Good. The Kobans have studied for thousands of years the ways of humans, and the ways to repair the damage done to Earth. When they rise, they will bring their wisdom and their limitless healing powers. When the battle is won, they tell me their first desire is to heal my own eyesight, which Tronot destroyed in a Greed King Torture Chamber. I promise you it's a good idea to avoid the 'TC.'"

Everyone gasped to think of this beautiful, gentle woman being tortured and blinded!

"I will be fine," Ulena promised her young, empathetic athletes. "If their torture served no other purpose, it firmed my resolve to destroy them with our light. We can win this, and we will."

Todd asked, "If the Kobans care so much, why did they let half of Earth get destroyed by Gonaquadet?"

"Gonaquadet was a massive meteor predicted for thousands of years. Its destiny was Earth, and could not be altered, not by anyone except God. God chose not to change Gonaquadet's destiny, and I cannot tell you why. Cataclysms have destroyed civilizations many times throughout the history of Earth, and the cataclysms always come when the people forget their own history, and their own inner powers. Gonaquadet was the same size as the meteor that completely obliterated the dinosaurs, yet humanity was not obliterated. Why? Perhaps—and this is only a guess—we have more work to do on this Earth before our race moves into another dimension, as the dinosaurs have."

I frowned. "Ulena, excuse me if this is a really dumb question, but I'm looking around, and all I see is eighteen crippled people in wheelchairs, and, no offense, but, our leader is a beautiful lady who cannot see. I mean, we don't look like what I would picture as the world's most powerful army. You know?"

Ulena smiled. "Ah, but you are! Physically gifted athletes with severed spines have been found to be most receptive to inner Earth's all-powerful electricity. Ley lines—the cracks in the earth's surface leading to her huge, energetic core—respond best to the cracks in your spines. Trust me, we have spent thousands of years researching this. The powerful energy at the earth's core will feed you, better than it can feed anyone else. That's your physical strength.

"Spiritually, and emotionally, each of you was the very best athlete in your field before your injury. You know what it is to push your bodies beyond what is thought to be their greatest limitations. You are the ultimate risk-takers, and it is because of your willingness to push to the limit and take huge risks, most of you were injured.

"Because you don't believe in limitations, you are the obvious choice for the Earth's biggest battle, because this battle will take place far beyond the confines of linear time and space. This battle will be

fought in inner space, as well as outer space. Only the greatest athletes would be mentally and emotionally capable of the journeys of
the inner mind and soul you are about to take. For the work required
in outer space, we have able-bodied astronaut warriors from the
planet Zoloat to do the physical work of slashing the Greed Kings'
Power Transfer Hoses. Your work will be largely spiritual, but I
promise you, you will go where very few Earth mortals have ever
gone.

She paused, and her gentle forehead folded into a sorrowful
frown. "The bad news is, some of you may die. Our goal is to wage
this battle without taking one single Greed King's life. Their goal is to
kill every one of us. For those of you who survive, in a world with the
Kobans living above to heal and teach us, all things are possible.
Motivation is also part of why you were chosen. There's a good
chance you will be perfectly healed, and fully able-bodied, when the
battle is won."

Todd laughed, and the darkness in him lifted for a moment. "Sign
me up, Ulena!" We all shouted in agreement.

Ulena's smile radiated throughout the golden-domed hall. "Each
of you will have a Mentor, but before you enter the Mentors' Chambers, I want to show you the kinds of journeys you'll be taking. We're
going to do a practice journey, the kind of travel our ancestors in
Atlantis and Mu often enjoyed. See how you like this kind of travel!
Our first astral journey begins, as all journeys begin, with complete
relaxation. So breathe in…"

Ulena's beautiful voice guided us into a deep state of relaxation,
using only our breath. Deeper and deeper we breathed, until her
magical words took us on a long journey that's hard to describe. In
astral travel, you really feel as if you are traveling, and you really "go"
there, but not in an airplane. Your mental powers take you there, but
you're not just there in your mind. According to Ulena, if you smell
things, your body is really there.

I first went inside a volcano. Many smoking craters left from Gonaquadet still pockmark Earth. It happened very suddenly. I took the form of an owl: a beautiful, strong-feathered owl, and as I became her, I felt the strong muscles in my back and wings flexing. Exhilarated, I pushed with these muscles upward, harder and harder. How glorious to feel my body exerting itself again! My abdominal muscles strained hard to get my body even higher. My muscles burned as I pushed them to rise and rise.

Once in the air, I felt the vastness of the sky all around me. I was afraid for a moment, afraid to be so tiny in such a huge, airy ocean. Afraid I would fall, but only for a moment, because once the realization hit me that I was truly in control of my owl-destiny, I was free. Never in my life—not before or since my accident—had I ever felt so free. I whooped loudly, and some strange owl-noise of pure elation came from my mouth.

Someone was trying to distract me from my bliss. I turned my attention to the ground. Someone was calling me loudly in my head, and I followed the vibrations of this message. Down, down I descended, hesitating only a little when I learned my destination was the inside of a belching, red volcano.

"Can I just go through molten lava like this?" I asked in my head, knowing I would be answered. I thought my questions, and "spoke" in my head: "I'm fond of these feathers, especially since this flying thing is new to me, and I think it's the feathers holding me up. I'm afraid they'll get singed, and I'm afraid of getting too crispy if I fall into that lava."

I could feel the sender of the messages smiling. "You will feel nothing except more freedom. Go through the lava, into the heart of the volcano. You will find us there."

I took a deep breath, and decided to believe. The worst that could happen was my death, and I didn't feel afraid of death. It was not my time. So I dove into the belching smoke and flames and lava. My message-sender was right: I felt only an intense, earthquake-like jolt, maybe like a seven on the Richter scale. I'd been trained for astral journey, and smells telling me I'd arrived. True to Ulena's prophecy, the smell of sulfurous gases surrounded me. There was no heat, however. I continued diving, through several jolts, until I came to the bottom of the volcano's source.

I found myself in an earthen pit, shaped like a bowl. The smell was musty, and it was a smell that made me feel I was in a place that was ancient, quiet, and dark. Above me, everything was loud and explosive, like a war movie, but here, the air was cool and still. The entire bowl of earth, and the rock surrounding me, glowed with vivid, red light. Feeling peaceful and safe, I noticed my wings had vanished. Oh, how I missed them, until I realized I was standing on my own legs! I was draped in a beautiful, garnet-red, silk dress. I felt beautiful.

Two people watched me with gentle expressions. The first, a beautiful black woman with wild, moon-white hair to her waist, wore a long, flowing, white dress. A cobra-shaped, golden crown rested on her head, and around her neck, a small, albino boa constrictor lazed. The snake massaged her long neck. She stood beside a handsome man. Tall, this white man with glowing green eyes would be referred to as a "major babe." A baby cheetah perched on his broad shoulders, watching me with luminous, blue eyes.

"Hi," I said, feeling immediately lame.

They both smiled. They loved my lameness. "Pepper," the woman said gently, and within myself, I suddenly knew her name was Lillith, and she was from the Land of Mu. (She was not wearing a nametag; I simply knew.) "Enjoy the journeys. Never fight them. They are journeys for knowledge, and journeys for love."

"Am I going insane?" I asked. "I mean, if I am, it's okay, because this is way fun. I love flying, and I love standing again. But I'd like to know the truth if I'm losing it."

The gorgeous man's green eyes glowed. His name was Bromand. "No, Pepper. You are journeying toward the truth: toward your past, your planet's past, and toward your planet's future. Your heart is pure, and hundreds of thousands of people have shot pure love into you. Love is the ultimate power, and that is why you are here. The love of all those people has given you the power to heal the world.

"We are your guides. Lillith is from the Land of Mu, known as the Land of the Immortal Serpent, and the Empire of the Sun. She is your ancestor, and she, like you, has seen the Earth in cataclysm. I am also your ancestor, from Atlantis. We will guide you and the people of Earth to the next phase, the phase of Peace and Harmony. All of us have waited thousands of years for this glorious time in our planet's history. You will feel our presence during crucial moments in the battles to come. We will give you strength.

"Several ancient clans will come together to make the Great Event: the Awakening of the Sun Quartz Fields. You, of the Clan of the Fan-Feathered Brow, will lead. Mother Ibis and the Egyptian priestess, Nanu, are your ancient mothers. The owl is your totem, and Caleina your source of totem power on this continent. Your great army cannot lose."

"Wow." I was not in an eloquent mode, and that was all I could say, but before I could recover, and maybe ask some intelligent questions, I was in the owl-body again. My strong stomach and back muscles lifted me above the frothing lava and smoke and flames. My body was jostled as it surged through exploding gases and rock. I rose and rose, aching with the effort, until I was high in the vast sky again. I flapped my outspread wings, simply for the joy of flapping against the wind. My owl-heart raced with the exhilaration of athletic exertion. My bird-heart grinned. I did somersaults in the sky, and swooped downward, then shot upward again. I reveled in the dizziness this new exertion brought me. I could have stayed up there forever, but it was not to be. My bird-self flew into the golden-domed hall, and into my regular, paralyzed-Pepper body.

Darn! The wings evaporated. No big "morphing" process took place as in the ancient "Animorph" stories. I'd often watched that old show as a child in the Earth Core tunnels. The kids acted like they were going to vommit when they morphed into animals. With me now, I was just poof, inside another form, body and soul.

Back in my chair, I sat, stunned. My body hurt, and my heart ached. I missed my wings, and the old, athletic sensations! What did all this mean? Lillith and Bromand had indicated this was only my first journey; I took comfort from that. Perhaps that meant my life from now on would be one adventure after another.

"Wow," Todd whispered to me. "Could you believe that astral-travel thing?"

"Very cool," I agreed.

Ulena was saying softly, "come back, come back, my warriors."

I felt a little woozy, but excited and happy, too. Ulena told us we would meet our mentors soon. I fidgeted nervously.

"Each of you has an ancestor who has chosen to come forward to train you," Ulena was saying. "Pepper, your Mentor-ancestor is Nanu, the First Mother of the Clan of the Fan-Feathered Brow. An Egyptian priestess who was murdered six thousand years ago, she was buried alive in the Hall of Records, beneath the rear paws of the Sphinx. It is said by the Egyptians that when the Sphinx imploded in 2014, they saw a vision of Nanu rising up and beckoning them. Egyptians say it was she who showed them where to dig to find the Hall of Records, and when they entered, there was her body, completely preserved, lying in state. They say her spirit wept at the sight of it, and when her tears reached the body, the body vanished."

I asked, "Are they like ghosts, these mentors? I mean, my mentor's been dead six thousand years. How do you guys manage her coming back to teach me all these things?" I guess I was the one in charge of asking the obvious, but I have no problem asking really elemental questions.

Ulena beamed at me. "Thank you, Pepper. I was hoping you would ask. We have always known that people who have unfinished business here on earth at the time of their death keep their souls outside a new body until their business is finished. They 'hang around,' as you might say, and, yes, they are referred to as 'ghosts.' We have devised modern techniques to be with them, and we have these spirits' full cooperation. We use their DNA to recreate and project their essence, to help them attend their unfinished business. You will meet Nanu, and see a projection of her life, her lessons, and what it is she wants you to do. We chose Nanu, because she is your Clan's First Mother, but also because the spirit of the man who murdered her and her husband has reincarnated into the body of Tronot, the Emperor of all the Greed Kings. Her personal motive—beyond saving Earth—is as fierce as mine, I assure you."

"Whoa!" I suddenly felt very important, but also not quite prepared for going up against the Emperor of the Greed Kings with a ghostly mentor.

Ulena turned toward Todd. "Todd, your Mentor-Ancestor is Swergen, First Father of the Clan of the Frozen Fields. He is an ancient Norseman who inherited all the fierce, magical powers of the runes Odin scooped up when he sacrificed himself on the World Tree. This will be a terrible responsibility for you, but we know you are up to it.

"Swergen was a great explorer of the icy, northern seas during Scandinavia's Bronze Age, about 1500 B.C. He was married to a volva, that is, a seer priestess named Ola, and she bore him a beautiful babe. She possessed the ancient runes of Odin, which had been handed down through her mother's mothers. While Swergen was off exploring and trading in his ship, his beloved Ola was murdered. It is said she came to him in a dream while he slept, weeping in grief for her motherless babe. She told him where to find the ancient runes, and that their babe would be safe, awaiting him. The evil one who'd tried to steal them had gone to lift the bag of runes, but searing poisons rotted both of his hands instantly. He died an excruciating death, and the runes mysteriously disappeared until Swergen found them, buried in a holy alder tree Ola the volva had described. He rescued their child, who lay there peacefully waiting, as Ola had promised. But you will learn this and more when you meet Swergen in the Mentors' Chamber. We chose Swergen because, of course, he is the First Father of the Clan of the Frozen Fields, but also because the spirit of the Evil One who killed his wife has reincarnated into Grobault, Leader of the Zombie Ghouls."

Todd's mouth hung open, hearing this history. "I don't know, Ulena. This Swergen guy doesn't sound like someone who'd ask a gimp like me to help."

Ulena's blind eyes watered sadly for a moment, but then her voice grew firm. "You must get over this self-pitying view of yourself as a gimp, Todd." She took a deep breath, as if to say, "and that is all there is to that." Ulena's breathing is powerful, because Todd straightened his upper back and quit his "poor-me" face. His face grew fierce.

Ulena, pleased, continued. "You'll need your hockey stick, and I think you'll enjoy ridding us once and for all of these ridiculous blights on our world." She smiled, and Todd grinned widely when she said it. "You will blast them into the center of the Sun Quartz Fields precisely as the Light Beings awaken."

"Cool. So where are the Greed Kings?"

"They are everywhere! Their driving force is Desire for Ultimate Power over Power. Where most of the survivors of Gonaquadet emerged with the desire to love and seek peace with their brothers and sisters, the Greed Kings saw the devastation as an opportunity to rule what was left of a ravaged world. Unfathomable piles of money aid them at every turn, but we in the Wisdom Palace have what they cannot have, for all their money and power."

"What is that?" Todd asked. Fully alert, he perched like a cat, ready to spring into action.

"You will begin to learn that in the Chamber of Mentors. Speaking the words might be dangerous. Soon you will learn all, and you will learn from the ones we trust. Queen Rona and Marla the Sea Faerie have spent thousands of years watching, choosing, and waiting for this moment in our planet's destiny. And now it is time."

At those words, the Palace shook. Our wheelchairs suddenly rose in the air, and each one of us floated in a single shaft of radiant light, toward a golden door.

"This is so fun!" I shouted at Todd.

MEETING NANU, FIRST MOTHER OF THE CLAN OF THE FAN-FEATHERED BROW

From the Earth Memories Archives
Compiled by Pepper McCullah
Clan of the Fan-Feathered Brow
Earth year 2030

Each one of us had our own golden door, so each one of us would be spending time alone with our personal mentor. I waved goodbye to Todd, knowing he was off to learn from his ancient Norse mentor, while I was off to be with my Egyptian-priestess mentor.

The massive, golden, door-in-space opened onto a beautiful floating garden. A small stream trickled musically over rocks, and pink and white lotus flowers bobbed in the water. The banks of the stream were carpeted with red and pink and blue flowers. Hummingbirds sipped from the flowers' nectar, and a couple tiny frogs leaped onto the rocks' moss. Slender trees I'd never seen loomed over the stream. The stream fed a quiet pool at its center.

Suddenly, as I peered into the quiet pool, a beautiful lady emerged. I recognized her immediately as my ancestor. It was so incredible; she looked like me! She even had the same, feathery eyebrows I have. Her dark eyes looked deeply into me, with love and recognition.

"Are you Nanu?" I asked, even though I already knew.

She smiled. "Yes. I am. It is good to meet you, my distant descendant. I have been waiting a long time. There is so much to say."

She sat beside me, in an Egyptian, King Tut-kind of chair that materialized out of nowhere, and I stared at her. She was an ancient version of me: long, black hair, big eyes—hers were black, and mine are green, but their shape is the same. Her skin was the color of dark honey.

She read my thoughts. "Date honey," she said, in a smiling voice. I smiled back at her.

"I can't believe it! You have the same feathery eyebrows everyone always glamorizes when they write about me in magazines."

"Oh, that is a very important part of who we are, Pepper. We belong to the 'Clan of the Fan-Feather Brows.' You were born with yours, and they have been handed down to you for thousands of years. I had to earn mine. They come from a magical bird, the Owl, universal symbol of spiritual wisdom. One great owl, Caleina, took me in her breast feathers, and she flew me to your world of mountains, to show me the place you would be born, thousands of years after I lived and died."

Nanu has the same, pretty mouth I have; I'm glad for my big lips and big teeth. She is older-looking; well, duh, she's 6,000 years older, so she should look older! I am talking about sorrows that made her face look weary.

"I turned into an owl, my first journey! No coincidence, right?"

Nanu smiled. "A coincidence is when things fit together perfectly. The owl is the totem of the Clan of the Fan-Feathered Brow. 'Totem' is the word Wisdom Keepers on this continent use to describe the special powers a certain branch of wise creatures gives you and your clan. Never forget that. When you face dangers—and there will be many—if you call Caleina to you, you will suddenly be filled with the powers of an owl. That is why you became the owl, so you would know its powers, which are full inside you, now."

I swallowed hard. So much to take in!

"I want you to see my life, and all that has happened," Nanu said, smiling. Honestly, I just wanted to sit and chat and be girlfriends with her, forever. But she was sitting back, eyes closed, smiling at my thoughts. She put her hand gently on my shoulder, easing me back into my wheelchair. We breathed deeply together, and I became incredibly relaxed.

A beautiful child laughed, and ran along a wide river. I knew instantly it was Egypt, because of the beautiful date palms overhead. Everything was deep green—Ireland green!—along the river, and then, about a mile out, everything was golden sand-colored: the sand, the houses, the land.

I watched, as if watching a movie (in my new life, I'd see a lot of these telepathic movies), as the beautiful girl flipped around in time to see the Nile Crocodile slithering up to eat the eggs of an ibis family. The brave little girl actually jumped onto the crocodile's back, smacking it with a rock, until it went underwater. Then came a big flash of light, and a flock of ibis lifted the girl. The girl-Nanu now glowed in the movie.

Nanu slept, and then a great, beautiful owl came into her room and lifted her, and her journey looked so fun, I was jealous! She was all cuddled into the owl's breast feathers as the owl flew her to my home in Lake Tahoe! The snowy top of Mt. Tallac shone brilliantly white in the starry night; the perfectly calm waters of the lake mirrored the great, white mountain. I gasped.

"The owl told me you would come from this place," Nanu said quietly.

Nanu's "movie life" continued. She became a priestess, and went to live in a long-since ruined temple dedicated to Isis in Dendera. She became an expert on the Egyptian god, Thoth, the ibis-headed god of knowledge. She learned great magic, passed down through priestesses since the "time before the great flooding," 10,500 B.C. (When the great island continent of Atlantis was destroyed, the ensuing earthquakes and tidal waves affected the entire world for quite some time. The sphinx at Giza was actually underwater for awhile! This was Noah's flood, and, millennia later, when Nanu won her feather brows, the sinking of Atlantis and the great flood time were still remembered.)

"Many of the Atlanteans had come from Mu, which sank 3,000 years before Atlantis. The Atlanteans knew, decades before it occurred, their island would likewise be completely destroyed, so they left in waves, scattering all over the planet. Each group carried the wisdom ways of the Lemurian and Atlantean cultures. Those who traveled to Egypt built the great Sphinx, in line with Leo in the sky, so they could be located by other Atlanteans and descendants of Mu, throughout the world. When the flooding had finally subsided, they built the Great Hall of Records beneath the Sphinx's rear paws. It was here I spent my happiest time on earth. But we are not there yet. I get ahead of myself in the story. We are still in the temple of Isis at Dendera."

I watched Nanu happily studying the wisdom of the Ibis-headed Thoth, God of Knowledge. I watched her working with the Divine Solar Eye of Horus the Sky God, and I watched her heal sick people: Nanu would go into a trance, and conjure the Divine Eye. I could see the eye, a huge, blue, green, and yellow eye. Glowing, it was almond-shaped, and rimmed in black Egyptian kohl. It hovered above her head awhile, then the sick person would get up and walk away.

I then watched Nanu invoke the goddess Isis—goddess of magic and love and restoration—and I watched Nanu invoke the 7 scorpions Isis used to heal and restore people. The scorpions shone, a rich, golden brown, and formed a huge, glowing circle about six feet above Nanu's head. Frankly, these seven ominous scorpions swimming above Nanu's head was a little creepy, until a dying child was brought before her. Nanu glowed, levitated, and a flash of light burst from above her head, where the scorpions swam. Light blasted into the dying boy's body, like a strong electrical current, and when the light faded, the little boy smiled, bowed to Nanu, and walked away.

Suddenly, the long, shadowy figure of a man who was clearly no good appeared in our movie. "Wow, Nanu, who is that skinny, dark-looking dude? He's watching you the way they do in horror movies. Ew, it's like he wants your body, the way he's looking at you. Lecherous jerk! Well, he doesn't just want your body. He wants your soul, and your wisdom. He wants to totally possess you!"

"Yes, he did. That is Memsek. He desired my body, and he hated that lust in himself. But what he most wanted was my wisdom. You are right. He wanted my soul. I was terrified of him, and rightly so."

Nanu uttered a little, sad cry. "Oh, Mantuk!" A handsome man appeared in the movie above our heads. "This man was my love, my husband, the father of my little Epu. Again, I get ahead of myself."

Mantuk was a major babe. Dark caramel skin, big muscles, tall, with a white, flashing smile. He came to Nanu in the temple at Dendera, and suggested he and Nanu go for a little carpet ride, sans carpet. What a line, only he followed up on it! Things were great, back then! Honestly, they just swooped up in the air, like in the animated Disney classics scientists took below to the Earth Core Tunnels before Gonaquadet. Nanu was pretty instantly smitten with this guy; who could blame her? All the while, though, there was a big, dark shadow on the ground: the shadow of Memsek.

There they were, Mantuk and Nanu, in the giant cave below the Sphinx, in the Hall of Records. Scrolls and tablets of stone lined countless shelves along the walls of the cave. Glowing crystal rocks of all colors shone everywhere in clusters, like crystal rainbows, on the ground, and on the big walls of the cave. The whole place was lit with this beautiful, glowing pink light.

"What is that glowing pink light?" I asked.

"Our source of power. We'll get to that. It's very important, and you'll learn all about it, eventually. But for now, pay attention," Nanu scolded, and I can't blame her, because she was reliving what must have been the greatest romance of all time.

She and Mantuk stared into each other's eyes. He took her hand, and gestured all around them in the cave. This was not even a PG-13 thing, though, because they were soon reading scrolls and tablets. Mantuk did perform a few really cool magic tricks; he waved his arms, and a flock of white ibis clustered. When they spread apart and vanished, a perfect little castle stood where the ibis had clustered.

Nanu gasped, and Mantuk smiled. He waved his arms again, and a fanciful, small, white horse appeared. Nanu's eyes bulged in wonder as the delicate, small horse approached her gently.

"The stylph. She is from Atlantis." He bent to pet the tiny horse, and she vanished.

"I want you to see Atlantis itself," Mantuk said, and he waved his arms. What a place! White marble buildings with beautiful columns, and the whole place reminded me of old photographs of Venice, Italy. The soil of Atlantis was red. The colors were red soil, white marble, purple flowers, and blue waters. Moats and canals wound beneath white marble walkways. Purple flowers were everywhere, in these big, giant, white marble urns. The streets were made of turquoise and yellow mosaic tiles, and beautiful, golden boats floated in the canals.

"This is so cool! And he just made that movie, like the one we're watching now!"

"Mantuk taught me to do this," Nanu quietly explained. "I was also very surprised, just as you are now. He asked me to live in the Hall of Records with him, and learn all the healing ways of Atlantis, and learn the magic for healing earth, and of course, I said yes."

Then, as Nanu was preparing for her wedding, just as we would, with a bunch of giggling, snorting girlfriends partying.

Memsek grabbed her, and took her in his arms. "Nanu, please stop this foolishness. I have waited my whole life to make you mine. I love you more than life, and only you can spare me from eternal darkness."

"Never!" The slender Nanu snapped at Memsek, spitting in his face. As she grew, he shriveled into a bitter, hate-filled man on the telepathic screen above us.

The wedding was incredible: set in the ancient temple at Dendera, with flowers, and dancers, and music. When Mantuk gently kissed his new bride, I swooned. Nanu swooned, too.

"You two were good," I said.

"We were."

The movie then moved to the Hall of Records, a huge cavern filled with Egyptian papyrus columns. Everything was lit with a soft, pink light. Nanu and Mantuk studied large, papyrus scrolls and stone tablets. Sick people came to them, and they invoked the scorpions, or the large golden eye of Horus to heal them. Nanu's tummy grew, and it was exciting to see Epu, her baby boy, be born again, millennia later, in our crystal bubble in the Mentors' Chamber. Gosh, he was cute!

"Epu, my dearest heart," Nanu murmured.

I noticed right away he had eyebrows shaped like feathery fans above his big, dark eyes. Adored by Mantuk and Nanu, he grew into a chubby little toddler. No ordinary toddler, he learned things quickly. He waved his chubby arms, and a kitten appeared before his delighted, sparkling eyes. I would have enjoyed watching a happily-ever-after fade-out here, but it was not to be.

On the riverbank, Mantuk pushed off the shore in his exotic, Egyptian sailing boat. He was waving goodbye to his beautiful wife and baby. Nanu was smiling, helping Epu wave his chubby little arm.

"He was off to visit with Atlanteans who'd settled in the islands far to the west—and show them what we'd learned. He never reached their shores."

Her voice choked. Mantuk, laughing and singing on the high seas, was overtaken by another Egyptian sailboat. Memsek's boat. Memsek wanted something from Mantuk, and they argued.

"I want the code to the knowledge of the Hall of Records."

"No."

"You will die."

Mantuk stood taller than Memsek, and raised his tensed, muscled arms to heaven. He yelled, and a flashing bolt of lightning seared the floor of the boat. Memsek jumped back.

"I will not give the code to one who is evil. The code is here, in this chest, and it is to be used for the good of Earth and humankind."

"I will take it after I kill you," Memsek responded.

"You will not understand it at all, Memsek, and you know that. The chest is worthless without me to translate the ancient languages of Atlantis and Mu."

"I will kill your wife after I've made her translate for me. She would do anything to save the life of her precious Epu."

"I know you are ruthless enough to do as you say. I always have known that about you, and so has Nanu. That is why I never taught her the code."

Memsek raised his black-robed arms, and produced an asp. The snake lunged at Mantuk, and bit his chest. "To the underworld with you, then!" Memsek screamed. "I'll translate it myself!"

Nanu turned away as Memsek shoved his dagger into Mantuk's gut. I threw my arm around her.

"I'm so sorry, Nanu. This must be awful for you."

"Yes. But you must know everything."

Ignoring the fallen body of Mantuk, Memsek frantically searched the boat for the treasure of ancient wisdom and knowledge. There was a huge chest, and he opened it. A faint, pinkish glow came from within the chest. His eyes lit up. His face actually glowed when he tried to read this one papyrus scroll. He put it down quickly, and his face contorted with fear. His large, frightened eyes bulged.

He was so excited, he didn't notice the flock of black-winged ibis swooping toward the boat. He called to the crewmen in his ship to come get the chest, but they recoiled from the menacing flock of ibis magically engulfing the boat. None of the crewmen would approach; instead, shouting in fear, they rowed away speedily.

The flock of ibis worked together to lift the chest, knocking Memsek into the sea. They flew away while Memsek cursed. He swam back to the boat and held on, still shaking his fist at the ibis. Mantuk's lifeless body was lifted by a dolphin, who started swimming.

I had a million questions. "Where did the dolphin take Mantuk? Where did the flock of ibis take the chest, and why didn't they just waste that guy, Memsek?"

"The chest of Knowledge was taken to the Shining Isles, what you now call the U.K., and the dolphin took my beloved's body to Alexandria, where I mourned him. Because Mantuk was a lector priest—a priest of learning and magic—and because he'd been a Kherep serquet—a scorpion charmer who magically reverses poisons in the body—he was given a ceremonial burial. A beautiful tomb was built for him.

"You ask why Memsek was not killed. The Knowledge was more important than Memsek, and he escaped. It is ironic: the only person who could have saved me from my death by poison was my husband, the Kherep Serquet, reverser of poisons. But he was dead."

My hand rose to my heart. "Oh, no! Memsek poisoned you? I thought you were buried alive."

"He poisoned me, but I was still quite alive when he buried me. He closed the Hall, which would be closed for millennia, until the great, 2012 earthquakes that would open it up."

"What about Epu?"

Nanu's expression softened, to one of joy and love. "Epu, my Sweetest one. Watch."

Nanu was in the Hall of Records, reading to her baby boy, when the same flock of black-winged ibis swooped into the glowing pink hall. They lifted Epu. Nanu was crying, but the great mother ibis, who was all white, looked at her with deep, loving eyes.

Nanu nodded, and spoke to her child. "Goodbye, my Epu. You will be safe.

Nanu's whole body tensed, and her eyes hardened. I saw determination and fear in those great, dark eyes. "I knew, of course, it was only a matter of time before Memsek killed me, so I worked furiously. One night, although I bolted and magically sealed the doors, Memsek was there, in my chamber."

"Nanu, love me. Don't make me do this."

"Kill me swiftly, Memsek, so I can be with my love."

"I need the boy."

"He is beyond your evil. You cannot touch him, and he will go forth, extending our Clan of the Fan-Feathered Brow. If it takes millennia for my clan to resurrect the old wisdom, it doesn't matter. It will be done. You cannot stop it."

Memsek approached her sadly. He bent toward her, wanting her to stop this terrible thing he was doing. "You will die, Nanu," he pleaded.

"I am not afraid of death."

"Your body is already filling with the poison."

"I know."

"Die, then! And know, as you die, that I am sealing this Hall of Records forever, for if I can't have the code of knowledge that lies in this hall, nobody can!"

"Yikes," I said softly. "Nanu, he's so evil! Has he really reincarnated into the guy I am supposed to fight?"

"Yes."

I shifted in my seat. I wanted to get the heck out of there. "You know, I am really not up to this. I am not as brave as you were. Memsek is not some tough opponent on the field. He's an evil, bad dude, Nanu. I'm a paralyzed football player! I'm not an Earth-saving hero, you know?"

Nanu smiled. "Oh, yes, you are. This is your destiny, just as mine was to love a man and a baby, and die without them in my arms. My destiny was to save the Code of Knowledge, and I did. Do I look tough?"

With her slender form and beautiful, soft, dark eyes, she looked like an exotic, gentle deer.

"No," I answered.

"Try not to think about it. Just move from the heart. Always move from the heart. That's all any of us do when we triumph in our most demanding roles. We are performing from our center of greatness when we are moving exclusively from the heart." Nanu's form—the vision of her—started fading. She was smiling as she faded, and I knew her smile meant she believed in me completely. I felt exhausted. This was no typical day, rising up in the air to sit in a magical garden, so I could meet an Egyptian priestess who'd been dead for 6,000 years.

Slowly, gently, I started floating down, down in the shaft of light, until I was back into the golden-domed Hall of Athletes. All the other "wheelchair warriors" were floating into their places, and all of them seemed as wiggy as I was. Todd was beside me, as he'd been before.

"Intense day, don't you think?" He took my hand, and gently squeezed it.

I laughed. "How will we describe it to the folks back home?"

"They'd lock us up!"

"Do you think the President, and people in power, know what goes on here?"

Todd's brooding, dark insecurity had shifted during his visit with his Mentors. He sat tall in his chair, and confidently answered, "Yes, they know. They believe in us. I'm sure of it."

"Wow, no wonder the Chieffette wanted to be a Wisdom Retriever! Did you learn anything about the Wisdom-Retrieving part?"

He shook his head full of dark blonde curls. His blue eyes penetrated. "No. That's stuff we'll learn in our next visits with the Mentors. This visit was just to get to know them, and learn their tragic histories. Did you know that some of the first people to venture forth from the Land of Mu were white skinned blondes that went to the Norse countries?"

"No."

"My ancestry goes way back, Girl, just like yours."

"My mentor is so beautiful."

Todd smiled so I saw both his dimples. His eyes glazed as he said flirtatiously, "Let me guess. She looks just like you."

I blushed a little, something dark-skinned people aren't supposed to do, and something I absolutely hate doing. "Are you, like, flirting with me?"

His flirty smile widened. "No!" He lied. "My Norseman-Mentor, Swergen, looked a lot like I look. Same blonde hair and blue eyes, same shaggy eyebrows. He was a good-looking guy, but it was a little creepy. He said I am his descendant from the volva-priestess, Ola, who was murdered. She hid my great, great, great grandfather in this magic alder tree with the sacred runes, and Swergen found him, perfectly unharmed, watched over by warm spirit-winds from the south. He says he was clutching the sacred runes and laughing, playing with them, like a rattle, when he reached the alder tree. Anyway, he says on our next visit, I'm going to start learning the ancient magic language of the secret runes. You're going to learn the secret energy code from Atlantis."

"How do you know my job?"

"I asked. We're all connected, Pepper. Saving Earth from total darkness is not going to be an easy task. It's just that you have the biggest, heaviest-hitting job. You're the one who's going to completely restore light and electricity to the world, using the ultimate renewable source. You're goin' to the Fields themselves, Babe."

My whole body shook with adrenalin: total fear ripped through me in one jolt. "The 'Fields?' What are they?"

"Pepper, it is so unbelievable. Up until now—for over 10,000 years—everybody thought Atlantis was a fairy tale."

"That is not true. Everybody's known about Atlantis all along. We just didn't discover the 'scientific proof' until 2012."

He shrugged. He was newly alive with excitement. "Whatever. But the Atlanteans had the whole energy thing completely wired, to use a pun. Your priestess used Atlantean light bulbs to light those caves, so everybody could see to paint all those great paintings inside the pitch—black tombs, back in Egypt. But when Memsek buried her in the Hall of Records, all that knowledge was lost. Until now. You are the one who gets to lead the charge to the Sun Quartz Fields, and light 'em up again."

"Why do you know so much more than I do?"

He grinned so both his dimples showed. "No offense, but I pay closer attention to things. I ask more questions."

"You are so full of yourself!"

"So. What's not to love?"

"Eew!"

Todd's news alarmed me, and my heart raced with fear. I was exhilarated, however, by all that he'd told me. Our lives would never be ordinary, from this point.

Ulena beamed at all of us, and told us to close our eyes and give thanks for all we'd experienced.

"Go home to the family who loves you, for you will not be with them too much longer. Return to your ordinary lives, and appreciate those lives for what they are: your ordinary lives are building your strength. Go in peace, my warriors."

WHICH ORDINARY LIFE MIGHT THAT BE?

From the Earth Memories Archives
Compiled by Pepper McCullah
Clan of the Fan-Feathered Brow
Earth Year 2030

My "ordinary life," as Ulena referred to it, no longer seemed to be quite the same. For instance, I went to see Frank, my Physical Therapist, and it was really hard when he asked, what was new, not to say, "well, I floated up in my wheelchair to this magical garden to visit with this Egyptian priestess who's been dead for 6,000 years, and I'm going to solve the whole earth's energy crisis by traveling to these Sun Quartz Fields, and, hey, what's new with you?"

Frank's freckled face reddened when he saw me. He took a deep breath, and exploded. "What the heck did you think you were doing, filling up my brand new Volkswagen bug with seaweed? It smells, and it's really ugly. Wheelchair or not, you're going to have to clean it up. Right now."

"Frank, I have no clue what you're talking about. How would I get seaweed? I live in Lake Tahoe, an hour from the beach."

"Maybe it was on sale in the Wisdom Palace, Ms. Wisdom Retriever. All I know is, you're cleaning it up."

"Frank, you don't have to get so testy. I didn't do it, but I'll clean your darned car."

"Oh, right, you're innocent, but there's a nice little card with your signature, 'Pepper McCullah,' on it."

"Yikes! What is going on?"

TROUBLE IN KOBA

From The Koba Memories Archives
Compiled by Marla, Sea Faerie
Keeper of Memories

Far beneath the squabbling young Earth heroes, an angry tremor shook the dreamy, liquid world of Koba. King Kanta's huge, angry feet pounded the ocean floor.

"Marla! Come to me at once!"

I tried to hide, knowing it was useless.

Spineless, floating Sea Urchins—the lime-green snitches!—found me, and gently pushed me toward the King. I was shaking as I approached our King. He is about eight feet tall, and his long, white hair drifts like a cloud all around him. His dark eyes blazed angrily in his enraged, purple face.

"Marla, why are you trying to cause all this trouble for Pepper, who has been chosen, down through the millennia, to save Earth?"

"Why, King Kanta, whatever are you talking about?"

"Marla, who else would paint a sea faerie on the side of the White House, and fill a physical therapist's car up with seaweed? Why are you doing these childish, stupid things?"

My sadness filled me, and spilled onto the ocean's floor. Tiny white sea-lilies sprang up where my tears fell. I could not think of a lie, so I told the truth. "King Kanta, my Queen abandoned me in her heart for that awful Pepper, and I am so jealous!"

Kanta began to stamp his feet and roar like a wounded whale, but our gentle queen put her hand on his strong, muscled chest. His response to his beloved queen's touch was immediate. Like a quickly spent summer storm, he calmed.

"Marla, Marla, my Dear One. Come here," Queen Rona said to me, motioning.

I love it when she talks to me as if I am a beloved child. I obeyed her. I sulked like a child as I sat on a softly cushioned stool at her feet, and curled toward her while she spoke.

"Marla, you are a peer…"

"Queen, I am not! You are three thousand years older!"

"What are 3,000 years when we're talking about thirteen millennia, Marla?" She laughed, that splashy, rainbow-colored, tinkly laugh I love so well. Queen Marla is the most beautiful woman in the whole universe, with black hair to her feet that swirls like the ink cloud of a squid whenever she moves. Her black eyes are massive, and glow like radiant coals. Her smile reached into my heart, and healed, and warmed me.

"Darling Marla, how can you feel you are replaced, when there has never been, nor never will be, anyone quite like you? Oh, Marla."

She held me close to her, and I smelled the wondrous Oil of The Sea Rose she always wears. It is nutmeg-spiced, and sharp like oranges, but rounded with a deep, red-rose fragrance. Whenever I smell the Oil of The Sea Rose, I see in my head Rona in her amazing underwater garden, lovingly tending her giant, cabbage-sized roses and tuberoses.

"I am sorry I hurt you by becoming so enamored with Pepper. I didn't see how it hurt you. Pepper is like a new puppy, a baby, for me. A great-great-great granddaughter. You are my friend, a woman friend, one of my dearest friends. We are in this together, my Dear One, together and forever. Pepper and I won't win without you. You must know that."

"I know."

"And you have done an extraordinary job, down through the millennia, recording the history of the Clan of the Fan-Feathered Brow. Do you have the whole history, that I may read it now?"

"Yes."

Queen Rona smiled; she was pleased. From her mouth came a tiny cloud of liquid rainbow—that is her happy response when she is pleased—and I watched it swirl above her eyes. The colors were swept into the inky folds of her cloud of black hair until they vanished. Rona continued.

"And you're certain that Alaiya has pieced together the Clan's history, to bring Pepper completely up to date, someday quite soon?"

"Oh, yes. Alaiya had a lot of time when she was down in the Earth Core Tunnel Palaces. She knows her entire ancestry, and she retrieved a lot of the ancient wisdom during their time beneath the earth."

"Let me see it, dear Marla."

"Yes, my Queen."

THE CLAN OF THE FAN-FEATHERED BROW A HISTORY OF MEMORIES COMPILED BY MARLA, SEA FAERIE KEEPER OF MEMORIES

I have written extensively of the moments initiating the Clan of the Fan-Feathered Brow, and Nanu of Egypt. My text has won great praise from the Queen and King of Koba. This, then, begins the volume telling of Nanu's descendants.

Nanu, the Clan's First Mother, bore Epu, with Mantuk. After Nanu's and Mantuk's murders by Memsek, Epu was raised on the island of Philae—the Jewel of the Nile—by a flock of black-winged ibis. The boy was kept hidden from Memsek, who lived far to the north in Egypt, near Giza. Priestesses from the ancient Temple of Isis at Philae tended to Epu. He lived in a magical, heart-and-mind realm of Wisdom, learning to always keep his heart open in the ways of ancient Mu and Atlantis. He communicated with crocodiles and scorpions and cats, and, of course, with the ibis birds who cherished him. He learned to fly with the black-winged ibis, and caused great worry among his magical bird and priestess family, flying all over Egypt at night.

The priestesses taught him of his brave parents, and he grew to become a wise, kind, handsome man with fan-feathered eyebrows. He had great healing powers, and was always happy. It is said of Epu that he always felt his mother and father in his heart. Many pilgrims who rowed out to the island of Philae in those days came to see the magical Epu to be healed, but the priestesses shooed them away. Too much danger existed that Memsek would find him. As the disappointed pilgrims rowed away from the island, Epu would open the light of his heart onto the pilgrims without their seeing him, and the pilgrims would be instantly healed. A priestess who once peeked from behind a wall witnessed such a healing, and she spread the legend that a bolt of greenish white light shot from his heart directly at the pilgrim, and above Epu's head floated the ibis-headed Thoth, emerald green, and Isis in white and gold, surrounded by her seven scorpions.

Attended by many black-winged ibis birds in a mystical ceremony, Epu was married to a priestess who traced her ancestry directly back to Atlantis. Nanu's great mother, the white ibis, presided. Epu's bride's name was Rakani. They pledged to the Keepers of Wisdom that, no matter how many millennia were necessary, their clan would search and find the ancient wisdom lost with Epu's mother Nanu.

Epu and Rakani studied in hiding near Philae, in an ancient wisdom school passed down from Mu to Egypt. They learned the secrets of heart, spirit, and mind over matter, and passed on their wisdom to other, underground schools. They bore six children, but only one, their son Aptara, bore the fan-feathered brow.

Far to the north, Memsek finally died of a scorpion's sting. This Keeper of Memories enjoys the delicious irony that he who murdered the Kherep Serquet [the scorpion charmer and reverser of poison, Mantuk] was killed by a scorpion! With the danger of Memsek gone from their lives, Epu, Rakani, and Aptara were free to travel about Egypt with their magic and wisdom. They became celebrated healers; Epu, like his father, became a Kherep Serquet who rescued more than one pharaoh from death by poison.

The clan continued, and I have the list of each wearer of the fan-feathered brow, but for brevity's sake, I mention only the most notable of them. For a time, the clan lived on the island of Crete, worshipping the snake-bearing goddess, and Isis in her varying forms. Fan-feathered brow members pushed east from Crete, all the way into Nepal, to learn from the Buddha's perfect wisdom. Millennia passed, and a Greek woman bearing the fan-feathered brow, Martis, followed the grace-laden path of Jesus, studying His perfect wisdom.

The clan seemed never to produce barren offspring, so the line continued, unbroken. Besides their obvious similarities, appearance-wise, they all possessed heightened spiritual awareness for their times, especially as the Civilization of Materialism gathered momentum. The Clan of the Fan-Feathered Brow always led scholarly or spiritual lives; many were healers. All avoided war and disease, and, miraculously, all found loving soulmates. Their successful marriages alone make theirs an extraordinary clan in the history of fickle humans.

One other thing they shared: the clan never seemed to be poor. They were not among the wealthiest of their times, but were always comfortable, and well provided for. We who study human history have learned how difficult it is to follow inner wisdom when survival is a struggle. For the Clan of the Fan-Feathered Brow, the study of inner wisdom has been a burning need, down through the millennia.

The clan was blessed, in many ways, and the great mother ibis, although never interfering, always kept her loving eyes watchful. One unlucky, non-Catholic intellectual, married to a fan-feather-browed woman—Anna—lost his head in Spain during the Spanish Inquisition. Anna, however, was bustled by the owl Caleina, through some dark, underground, aqueduct tunnels built by the Romans. Upon her arrival into the night air outside the fetid tunnels, a flock

of black-winged ibis, led by the massive Caleina, carried her to Alexandria, Egypt, where she married an Egyptian and bore a daughter
who wore the fan-feathered brow.

And so it went. The clan remained in Egypt through the centuries,
until the time of Raymond Browne, a British Egyptologist in the
1920's. It was an exciting time for a European to be an Egyptologist,
for Egypt had been rediscovered by Europe. Sand had been shoveled
away from the long-buried Sphinx, and diggers arrived. Raymond
came from a wealthy family, and was barely out of his teens when he
was initiated into the Hermetic Order of the Golden Dawn, an
English Rosicrucian society founded in 1888. Egyptian mysticism,
and wisdom handed down from ancient times, were his passions.

As soon as he gathered enough Golden Dawn expert archeologists
who burned with his same firey desire for knowledge, Raymond led
quite a large expedition to Giza, in order to prove a connection
between the lost continent of Atlantis and Egypt. (The idea of Atlantis had reawakened in the 1920's.)

While taking a restful break from his work at Giza, Raymond met
a beautiful, aristocratic Egyptian, Reina. Raymond was invited to
inspect the oldest ruins in Egypt—a temple to the Goddess Isis, quite
a ways south on the Nile, at Philae. Raymond became enchanted
with Egypt as the slow boat's oars plied the crocodile-filled Nile.

Reina greeted Raymond as he stepped from his boat onto the holy
isle of Philae. He was startled by her lovely eyebrows, which fanned
in an arch, like soft feathers, above her lustrous, dark eyes. Reina was
in charge of the restoration of the Temple of Isis on the island of
Philae, without ever knowing that her ancient, great-great grandfather had once been raised by the ibis birds and priestesses, there.

They made a beautiful couple, sharing the passionate excitement
of their discoveries of ancient history. Reina showed Raymond the
tiny island's vast history she'd unearthed in the rubble: a history of
changing conquerors and changing religions. Christians had demol-
ished the temple most recently, and Reina's task was to piece together

the Christian temple—which had been built upon the Isis Temple rubble—separately from the Temple of Isis.

I, watched while Reina slept on the island and was wakened by Caleina one moonlit night. Reina sat up and stared calmly into Caleina's deep, fierce eyes. Creating a vision in the moonlit island night as the Nile's waters lapped against the sand, Caleina showed Reina the story of her clan. After that, Reina was able to piece together her clan's history.

Raymond and Reina were married at the Temple of Isis on Philae, and the spirits of many ancestors with fan-feathered brows were present. It was a lovely wedding; Egyptian columns surrounded them, and beautiful date palm branches bowed in the breezes wafting from the Nile. They bore two sons, Edmund and Chad. It was Chad who inherited the fan-feathered brow, and who became Alaiya's beloved grandfather.

Chad grew up in England, but traveled widely with his parents, studying ruins and manuscripts that connected Mu and Atlantis with various countries' cultures all over the world. He inherited not only the fan-feathered brow, but the firey quest for ancient wisdom from his parents. He fell in love with India, and spent that country's tumultuous post-Independence decade, the 1940's, studying sacred wisdom texts in the basements of temples, and digging in the ruins of the great Indus Valley civilization. As a mortal during those years, I lived in Varanasi, and remember Chad's penetrating gaze and fan-feathered brows.

Like his father, Chad was fortunate to find a woman who shared his quest for ancient wisdom. Meena was a Hindu archeologist determined to prove that the Indus Valley civilization was connected to Egypt because of their shared ancient roots in the Motherland of Mu. Meena had read all of Raymond Browne's books, and Raymond and Reina welcomed her with open hearts.

Chad and Meena's marriage was a beautiful union of souls and minds. They bore only one son, shocking the local, Indian culture, where women bore enormous broods, but Meena's body was fragile. When typhoid fever swept through with the monsoon rains, one year, it took Meena. Her young husband wept his own monsoon, and prayed for death. Throughout the millennia, this moment of sorrow was the biggest threat to the Clan's unbroken line, for this poor man nearly wept himself to sleep forever.

Their three-year-old son, Rahd—named after Ra, the Egyptian (and Lemurian) God of the Sun—was sleeping in his netted crib while his father wailed and tore his hair in the next room. Rahd woke and cried, and the cobra snake must have smelled the tantalizing salt in the tears of the man and baby. The cobra slithered into the baby's crib in silence, meaning to make a meal of him. Suddenly, the room filled with golden light, and the large, white, great mother ibis lifted the baby. The cobra left in a thwarted huff, and the great mother ibis carried the babe in her soft wings.

She went to Chad, who thought he was dreaming. He opened his eyes to see Meena, radiantly bathed in white light, standing beside a giant white ibis who held their son. Meena lifted Rahd from the ibis' wings and handed him to her husband. For only an instant, he felt her hand on his cheek. She looked at him fully, with great love, before her image faded. From that moment, Chad became a devoted father. The bright-eyed boy became Chad's source of life and joy. Because of the miracle vision, Chad knew he must learn his history, and so he did: he learned the entire story of the Clan of the Fan-Feathered Brow.

Rahd and Chad were inseparable, studying the Indus River Valley in their mother's name. A quietly energetic twosome, they grew excited over books and shards the way other fathers and sons might cheer athletic games.

In 1962, the Clan of the Fan-Feathered Brow finally landed in America, as Caleina had long ago assured Nanu they would. Chad, a distinguished archeology photographer, was hired by the prestigious National Geographic Society, and he and Rahd settled near Washington, D.C. Rahd, sixteen, wore dark skin during a time of racial tension in America, but Rahd shrugged when he met with prejudice.

Rahd gravitated toward Eastern religion, which for him seemed both an awakening and a way to know his long-dead mother. He learned the arts of ancient wisdom that have been lost and rediscovered so many times: mind and heart over matter.

Sandy was working in a meditation retreat center when Rahd smiled at the pretty blonde woman with green eyes. The tall, handsome Georgetown University freshman with eyebrows that fanned like feathers above his big, dark eyes asked her for some tea. She was two years older than Rahd, and studying geology and religion history. Their combined enthusiasms united them; Rahd became excited by the Anasazi "Ancient Ones" and the Lemurian spiritual beliefs they'd handed down to the Hopi and the Navajo. Sandy studied the stories buried in ancient strata. Their wisdom journeys led them to the Southwest.

Alaiya was born in 1976, in a cave that had been an Anasazi family home three thousand years before. The indomitably athletic Sandy and Rahd had been cross-country skiing through a deserted Mesa Verde National Park when Sandy's contractions began. The baby was not due for two weeks, so Sandy thought nothing of it, and continued with her business of rock collecting and study. When a pain ripped through her, she screamed.

Just outside the park, a Navajo woman was outside, feeding her goats, when she heard the scream of a woman very close to her birth time. The woman ran inside, grabbed some towels, blankets, and a ceremonial knife handed down from generations. She shouted orders to her son. He was to follow her into the park with a bucket of hot water.

The baby was eager to greet the crisp, blue sky of southwestern Colorado. The light was silver and gold outside the cave as Sandy panted. Rahd helped her breathe slowly, and held her hand. Years of meditative serenity did not prepare him for the panic he felt inside, yet he smiled calmly at his wife until she, too, was calm.

The Navajo woman appeared at the mouth of the cave holding towels and a knife, and Sandy would later tell her daughter how the woman's head was haloed in gold and silver light. In her delerium, Sandy smiled. An angel had come. The woman worked in silence at Sandy and Rahd's side, and she said nothing when a tall young man appeared with a bucket of hot water that sent clouds of steam into the wintry air. The sturdy, red woman grunted and spoke in Navajo, and smiled widely when Rahd responded in her language. She stared for a long time at his fan-feathered brow, and she seemed to know everything. A lifelong bond was forged between them.

The woman told Rahd, "The baby is early because she is eager. She is strong, and she will survive the purification of Mother Earth. She has a very big spirit that will be sung for thousands of years. She comes. Look! Her eyebrows are like the feathers of an owl, just like her Papa. She will be very wise.

"This is the Clan of the Fan-Feathered Brow. I come from the Clan of Rock and Sun. My clan and your clan will be together to greet the Final World after the New Dawn."

When Alaiya emerged, her head swiveled quickly to find her father. He later told his daughter, "You looked right at me, with a penetrating, knowing look. You searched my face for something, and you must have found it, for you then relaxed, and smiled. Your entrance was profound, for you came as a spirit with a purpose. I knew, in that one moment, the world and my life were destined for huge occurrences."

Rahd, Sandy, and Alaiya stayed in the Navajo midwife's tiny hogan while Sandy rested. The Navajo midwife immediately became known as "Noni"—Grandmother Pink Flower That Gives Life—and she buried Sandy's placenta in a beautiful spot and sang Navajo prayers to Mother Earth.

When Sandy was strong again, Noni blessed her grown son and told him the hogan was his. Her destiny was with this young family, the Clan of the Fan-Feathered Brow. Her son, belonging to the Clan of Rock and Sun, must live from his heart and meet their clan's destiny.

Rahd, Sandy, their baby, and Noni returned to the mountains of New Mexico, to grow, to learn, and to prepare.

Alaiya's life was a blessed one. Grandpa Chad became a fixture in the beautiful, mountaintop home. Alaiya would sit on his lap while he told her stories of Egypt and India. Alaiya learned from her grandfather the long story of the Clan of the Fan-Feathered Brow, and she memorized it. The characters lived in her heart, so she was never lonely, despite their isolated life. Love filled the mountaintop.

Alaiya learned the ways of the Navajo from Noni. Noni told Alaiya the story of her Navajo parents, and the Blessingway ceremony they performed on her when she rested in her mother's womb. "They decided at this Blessingway that I would be a great healer," she said. "In our culture, healers are taught when it is very quiet, inside the womb, where we can listen best. While I rested inside my mother, I learned everything about healing. I learned that healing is about balance. We are only sick when we are out of balance." Noni took Alaiya on long walks and showed her how to gather Navajo tea flowers, and willow bark for healing. Noni taught her that great Spirit Forces live in all things, and that Alaiya's mother Sandy was a great Spirit Healer of the Earth, because she understood the Spirit Force that lives inside each rock.

"In the great time of purification, your mother Sandy will teach survivors how to bless the spirit force inside each rock. This planet will survive because of spirit forces inside the rocks in the sky."

With her beautiful, blonde mother, Alaiya always felt useful, for Sandy always had a task for Alaiya that seemed important. They often climbed the limestone cliffs above their house, and Sandy would explain to Alaiya the age and secrets of the ancient rocks.

Alaiya loved her mother's green eyes, and the way they shone in sunlight. Alaiya had inherited them, and she was proud. Her mother's body was lean and hard from all her climbing among the rocks, and she always smelled of sage.

Alaiya's father, Rahd, was always smiling. He rarely spoke, but his heart was always open. She could feel it. Alaiya always felt peaceful and happy when she was with her father, but that was not often, for his meditation and his writing took most of his time.

Noni and Grandfather Chad were Alaiya's sun and moon. They doted on her. One day, when Alaiya saw Noni and Chad kissing, she knew her biggest dream had come true. Hers was a joyful childhood, spent in an intellectually and spiritually charged atmosphere.

The family lived in the high mountain wilderness outside the beautiful, tiny town of Los Ojos, New Mexico, a few miles south of Colorado's southern border. Los Ojos was made famous by the Jicarilla Apache, Navajo, and Ute artisans who lived there. Rahd and Sandy had worked with a local Navajo contractor to build a house that harmonized with the beautiful, high mountain surroundings. The house was built mostly of wood and glass, but magnificent boulders rested in the living room. The windows faced Los Brazos Peak, over eleven thousand feet high, and the family watched the seasons change on the mighty cliffs: from the greens and golds of spring and summer, to the rose and tangerine colors of autumn, to the white, swirling snows of winter. Alaiya was home-schooled by her illustrious parents and grandparents, and learned both modern curriculum requirements and the ancient ways of many cultures.

Alaiya never grew tired of hearing the legends surrounding the Clan of the Fan-Feathered Brow. Her ancestors' lineage was rich with tales of wisdom seekers' journeys: her clan was peopled with archeologists, scientists, explorers, and spiritual teachers. The Clan had roamed the continents, seeking wisdom throughout Africa, Asia, Europe, and now, America. Alaiya's youth was a wondrous one, but she'd also inherited her clan's thirst for journey and discovery.

At twelve, Alaiya was incomparably beautiful. Olive-skinned, she wore her dark, fan-feathered brow above the gold-green eyes she'd inherited from her mother. Her hair was a dark, chestnut brown.

Noni had taught her about the "Grandfather Herb" and exactly where it grew in the nooks of the limestone cliffs above their home; it was named because when Grandfather Chad was out of sorts, this particular bush helped balance his spirit. Noni, as a Medicine Woman of renown, knew that each person required an herb special to him, and it needed to be ground especially for the person, in accordance with the way the spirit was unbalanced.

Noni explained to Alaiya that Grandfather Chad was not feeling well, and Noni hated to leave him for even a moment. Noni's love for Chad filled the room in which he now slept, so with great reverence Alaiya left the house and put on her climbing shoes. It was a golden, crisp autumn day in the San Juan Mountains, and the hills glowed with tangerine-and orange-colored Aspen trees in the sun. Alaiya lifted her head to Father Sun in gratitude for the beauty of her life.

Her father was meditating, and her mother was lecturing at an Earth Sciences conference in Denver. It was a good day to hike alone in this magnificent wilderness. As she climbed to the niche between boulders where the tiny pink flowers of the Grandfather Chad herb grew, she gave thanks to Mother Earth for growing this medicine that would heal her beloved grandfather. A beautiful, silvery spider occupied the plant, so Alaiya asked her permission to only snip the outer flowers. She was very careful not to disturb the spider, who was, after all, a direct descendant of the Navajo's Grandmother Spider, also known as Thought Woman. Thought Woman had once thought the Earth, the sky, the galaxies, and all that is, into being, so Noni had taught Alaiya to be reverent of all spiders. Gently, Alaiya snipped the outer pink flowers, and put them into Noni's herb basket.

As she focused on snipping the flowers, she realized she was not alone. She sensed the presence of terrible danger nearby. Taught by her father to slow her breath whenever faced with danger, she took some steady, deep, "Perfect Breaths" from deep within her belly.

When a boy with a huge knife jumped from behind a huge, jutting boulder, she was ready. They were on a table-like precipice, and Alaiya very smoothly lunged sideways. Her young attacker fell into the air and plunged twenty feet. He rolled until a bush stopped him, on another limestone rock.

Alaiya's head spun, for the sky had exploded with blinding light. Surrounded by the flapping of wings, she saw the great white mother ibis of her ancestors. Her heart filled with joy at the magic of such an out-of-place bird here in the high mountain desert. Huge above her, the great mother ibis had vast, black-tipped wings and a long, glowing, golden beak. She spoke to Alaiya.

"I came to Nanu thousands of years ago when she rescued my offspring, and I rescued your father as a babe in his crib. You, Alaiya, need no rescuing, but I come to tell you that your visionary gifts will help preserve your world beyond the coming cataclysm. Your daughter will be the one who sets your people free forever. Your clan will unite with the other Clans of Light to free Earth people from their lives of suffering. Meet the owl Caleina, who carried Nanu to this land, long ago, and serves as your Mentor-Totem in these times. Never walk in fear, for if you trust your inner wisdom, all will be well."

Alaiya spoke. "Is the boy dead?"

Gently, the ibis answered. "No. Go to him, and show him your True Self. He will become your lifelong friend and brother." The ibis chuckled. "He lies there in shock, for this mountaintop glows. He has never seen an ibis, let alone a talking ibis. Caleina will take you to him."

Just as her ancestral mother had felt the softness of Caleina's breast feathers, in millennia past, so Alaiya now snuggled into the gigantic owl's breast feathers. The massive bird enfolded her, so her head was against the soft feathers covering Caleina's breast. She sank into the wisdom of the primeval song, the drumming of a great owl's heart.

Her attacker's face contorted in fear as the massive owl gently dropped Alaiya at the bottom of the cliff. He covered his head with his hands. He was shaking.

"It's okay," Alaiya said, soothingly. "No one is going to hurt you. I forgive you for trying to hurt me, and I choose you to be my protector and friend, for life." She placed her hand on the boy's sweating back, and felt the middle of his spine with her fingertips in the old Egyptian way, to learn his name was Chris.

Chris was ten. He'd thought Alaiya's herb basket had dope in it he could sell in town, so he'd tried to rob her. He was the son of a Vietnam vet who'd come to the San Juan Mountains to forget his pain. Chris' mother was from Mexico, and had run off four years ago with Chris' baby sister to escape her abusive husband.

"My life has not been so good," he told Alaiya.

"It is time to heal your life," Alaiya told him. "Come, be my little brother, but first, help me gather some willow bark for my grandfather."

Sandy and Rahd accepted the sandy-haired boy fully, in their home, and in their hearts. It was a happy time for Alaiya, as she continued her home studies with her grandfather, Noni, and Sandy. Rahd had become a celebrated spiritual teacher, whose books sold extremely well. A gentle soul who said little and smiled often, he spent a lot of time traveling to the borders of countries at war. There, with many others, he would meditate for peace.

He approached Sandy with a dream in his heart, and she readily accepted it into her own heart. They would build a retreat center, dedicated to building worldwide peace and cherishing Mother Earth. They would honor all cultures' ways of wisdom, and would work to remember the very ancient ways. Rahd and Sandy never spoke of their highest dream—to stave off the coming cataclysm with peace and remembrance, but each knew the other dreamed that highest dream.

For Chris, a world of light opened within him, as bright as New Mexico's own celebrated, physical light. His new family shared a gentleness he'd not experienced since he was six, when his mother left. He worked eagerly, building the retreat center, gathering herbs for Noni, and listening at Grandfather Chad's feet when Alaiya had her lessons. For the first time in his life, he was part of something beautiful.

"The Mountain Center for Universal Peace" brought people from all over the world. Students and teachers shared ancient wisdom and meditation for the three-or four-day retreats. Alaiya enjoyed the many visitors, and asked them about their lives at home. Sometimes, she would stay with a guest, talking long into the night about her own visions of life and the world.

When Alaiya was eighteen, she announced to her family that she'd applied to Stanford University. "I'd like to be out in the world, with people my own age," she said simply.

The next few months whirred for everyone. Chris and Sandy and Noni and Chad and Rahd watched through their tears as Alaiya took placement tests and wrote essays. Her distinguished grandfather's letter of recommendation was heartbreakingly beautiful, telling of his years schooling Alaiya in the sciences, arts, and letters. He wrote of their worldwide travels, and how readily Alaiya had understood each new culture in her heart. His letter was an encapsulated history of Alaiya's interesting, unusual life.

Though aching as she left her lovely mountain home, and her beautiful, illustrious family, Alaiya was also intoxicated with excitement. She believed the magical ibis: hers was a destiny vital to the planet, and it was hers alone. She must go find it.

She and Chris had never talked much about that day the magical ibis had lit the mountaintop, but they did, the night before Alaiya left for California.

"That giant bird who made the mountaintop glow—what it said to you is why you're leaving, right?" Chris asked.

"Maybe," Alaiya answered. "Chris, I know in my heart huge things will change the earth in our lifetime, and each of us has to make a difference."

Chris' big, dark eyes grew moist. "I know you have to go. I will miss you, and I will take care of your grandparents while you are gone. Thank you for rescuing me that day."

Alaiya's first days at Stanford University tested her will to go out into the world. She slept badly in the noisy world, and she found her peers just as impossibly loud. She missed her golden aspen-leafed mountains that autumn, and she would miss cross-country skiing in the white silence of winter in the mountains.

Her place of peace was in the water, in the University's enormous, 50-meter swimming pool. All her spare time was spent in the liquid silence of the pool, stroking gracefully, loving the feel of driving her arms through water.

She enjoyed her classes, and followed the passions of her clan. Her major was science, with a minor in religious studies. She gravitated toward astronomy, as a way to feel closer to the vast, brilliant canopy of stars above her mountaintop home in New Mexico.

Jim McCullah was her destiny, so it was no coincidence he was in both her astronomy class and her religious philosophy class. Enchanted by Alaiya, who hadn't noticed him yet, Jim started spending his lunchtimes in the swimming pool.

There had never been a man like Jim anywhere near Alaiya in her lifetime. Jim McCullah was Stanford University's star quarterback. Wherever he went, on a Monday after a football game, or on a Friday before a big game, Jim was stalked by television cameras as he walked to his classes. Young women smiled at him invitingly, but Alaiya's was the only smile he craved.

The plaintive stares Jim lavished on Alaiya, if not noticed by her, were noticed by others. Perhaps because of the star quarterback's absorption with Alaiya, other students were drawn to her. For the first time in her life, Alaiya had girlfriends her own age. Stanford was filled with very serious scholars, and her girlfriends were no exception, but when they put their books down, these young women giggled. They teased her.

One friend, Heather, tried to talk some sense into Alaiya during their short break between classes. "How can you keep turning down Jim McCullah? He's gorgeous, he's brilliant, he's nice, and he's got millions of dollars in pro football contracts wrapped up."

"He does seem nice," Alaiya said distractedly, smiling, "but I have no idea what to do. I'm a total country bumpkin, here, and I feel stupid and awkward around guys."

"Alaiya," Heather said warmly, "you don't need to <u>do</u> anything. You're beautiful, and he's crazy about you. Just let him talk. Guys aren't great listeners, anyway. They just want to talk."

"Really?"

"Absolutely," Heather assured her.

Alaiya thought about her own, isolated world. Her father rarely spoke, but her grandfather talked more than anyone. Chris sometimes annoyed her to death, he talked so much! "Two out of three talkers," she mused.

"Thank you, Heather! That makes it so much easier, if you're right. If you're wrong, though, he and I will just stand there, looking at each other."

"Trust me, he wouldn't mind that," Heather said with a sigh.

Emboldened by this information about men, Alaiya stood one day in Jim's path, and allowed him to approach her after their religious philosophy class.

"Are you going swimming today?" He asked.

"Yes!" She answered enthusiastically. This wasn't so hard.

"Me, too! Can I walk to the pool with you?"

"Yes!" She said again, even more enthusiastically. She could do this!

"What do you think about Maslowe's 'Peak Experience' idea?"

"I feel as if Maslowe knew me," she answered. For a moment, she was shocked she'd said so much. "I mean, I've felt that way so many times, at home, when the sun exploded colors onto the rocks at sunset, making them blush all firey. I felt so completely happy, I felt as if I could never get happier than that."

"Me, too, I feel I fully know the 'peak experience' thing—like when I throw long, and my receiver catches it. The whole world, and my whole life, feel perfect: the best it can get."

Alaiya smiled up into Jim's handsome, sunburned face. He had curly brown hair and freckles, and his hazel eyes were the color of a New Mexico fawn's fur in the sunlight. We are so very different, she thought, and yet, we are exactly the same.

He was strong, and he appreciated Alaiya's athleticism in the swimming pool. He had to work very hard to stay behind her. Finally, she slowed down, and he blocked her swimming path. He was breathing terribly hard.

"What are you, a marathoner?" Jim asked with a huff.

Alaiya laughed. She was not even breathing hard. "Altitude. I grew up at eight thousand feet elevation, in the mountains. It gives me an incredible advantage when I'm at sea level."

"I'll remember that. Maybe I'll train in the mountains, this summer," he said, looking deeply into Alaiya's green eyes.

Alaiya felt herself swoon. "Maybe you will," she said boldly, looking deeply into his fawn-colored eyes.

Alaiya and Jim were inseparable after that. Alaiya giggled. Her parents would be horrified to think of her with a football-player boyfriend. Despite herself, she loved the game: she loved watching strong young men run with all their hearts. She loved watching Jim raise his arm to throw to his receiver. She grunted when men were tackled, feeling their pain, but they never seemed to mind. In fact, they were like the many puppies at home in New Mexico: puppies loved tackling, and tumbling all over each other. While she watched

Stanford pummel Oregon State, she reflected she hadn't written her parents in a long time. She decided to mention her boyfriend in her next letter home.

Rahd and Sandy were horrified, and rushed, with Chad and Noni and Chris, to Stanford to meet Jim over Thanksgiving weekend. They stayed on the ocean, near Half Moon Bay. Noni delighted in seeing the ocean for the first time, but was deeply puzzled by the thick fog. Chris was amazed by the sea and the Stanford campus in Palo Alto. Chris was in awe of Jim McCullah, and was first wooed by Jim. They passed around a football on the beach, with Alaiya. Chris ran for touchdowns against Jim.

"I like him," Sandy told Rahd over her shoulder, as he came up behind her at the window.

"Then all of us will like him, eventually," Rahd smiled into her hair, which was now the color of wet sand. "You're never wrong about things, or people. Let's see if I can still catch a football," he said, and ran out onto the beach to join the others. Alaiya beamed at her father. Living a 'Peak Experience' moment, she had never felt happier in her life. Chad and Noni, watching from the window, smiled.

"This family is growing," Noni said. "Their babies will be strong."

"Let's not get carried away, Noni. They're very young," Sandy said.

Noni snorted. "Oh, he is the one. The Clan of the Fan-Feathered Brow does not dally with dating much." She smiled a wicked smile, and rested her weathered hand on Sandy's.

Sandy smiled widely. "No, we don't. Gosh, my baby girl. How did she get so big?"

"The Purification is coming. Mother Earth needs your baby's baby. Time is going faster, now, and gravity shifting. It is a faster time. An exciting time the Hopi talked about for thousands of years: the fast time before the purification."

Chad rose from the couch to take his beloved Noni's hand, and for once, was quiet.

That night, Rahd and Sandy dreamed together of the owl, Caleina, who told them Mother Earth depended on the Clan, and that all would be well. In their dream, Caleina opened her huge wings to reveal her thumping heart. It glowed, bright red, emanating with white and golden light that filled the room.

"Welcome him," she said with her deep stare.

Alaiya and Jim studied astronomy and science engineering and religious philosophy. They studied the sky, and they studied Earth. They spoke with Alaiya's family about their calculations: the Hopi, the Egyptians, the Mayans, and the Bible had predicted a comet would destroy Earth as we know it about in the year 2012. According to Alaiya and Jim's research, 6,000 Amor asteroids were due to cross the Earth's orbit in the next two decades, and one of them looked especially ominous.

"Purification is coming," Noni told Jim decidedly. "You will take the Clan underground."

Jim graduated from Stanford, and was the Miami Dolphins' number-one draft pick. If Alaiya found the heat and humidity of Florida unbearable, she never complained. She spent all her time in their large swimming pool. Their location made it easy for the two of them to spend their time off studying Mayan manuscripts that talked of "collisions in the heavens," and "the violence when heaven collides with earth."

Jim played professional football for eight years. He was the highest paid quarterback in history. In the beginning of his first season as a free agent, a bad concussion knocked him dazed for weeks. He and Alaiya agreed: it was time for him to quit. The time had come for Jim to work with Alaiya and her famous mother on Purification Countdown. Their first baby, Collin, was born in 2006, when Jim and Alaiya were thirty. A dark-haired baby with Jim's fawn-colored eyes, he did not wear the fan-feathered brow.

Alaiya loved being a mother more than she had ever loved any other part of her life. She found herself delighting in the most primal aspects of motherhood. She could spend her entire day sniffing her baby's scalp, or looking into his deep, wise eyes. Collin was an easy, happy baby who slept a great deal, so no one was surprised when Alaiya was pregnant again, shortly after Collin's first birthday.

In '07, two hundred scientists chose Lake Tahoe as one of the many places for the underground tunnels. Sandra Browne was asked to head the geological studies to pick the rock that might best withstand the magnitude of the coming comet's explosion. Sandy's responsibility was also to decide how deep to tunnel. As she watched Alaiya cuddle her new grandson, Sandy felt the pressure of all the ages come down on her. The crush of weight was sometimes so overwhelming, she was tempted to quit.

Noni was adamant she would not be going underground. "I want my body to be part of the Purification," she said.

The mountains were chosen because new mountain ranges would probably form—as they had, millions of years before, in other cataclysms—along the plains. It was best to go where non-volcanic mountains already existed. The Sierra Mountains were chosen because the plates beneath them tended to shift often and well. After all of Sandy's agonizing research, she decided they should go two miles down. Construction of the underground, Earth Core Tunnel palaces began. The Clan moved to the shores of Lake Tahoe.

Humankind's ingenuity can be dazzling, and no details were ignored. All waste would generate the hydrogen to feed the fuel cells that would give them light to grow their crops. Fuel cells' waste products are water and heat, so two miles below the earth's surface, they would all be warm, and their crops would be watered. The abundant plants growing everywhere, below, would give them oxygen.

In July of 2008, the relentlessly laboring scientists and engineers took a very short break from their all-consuming work to celebrate the birth of Sesheta Tsilkali McCullah, the heralded baby with the fan-feathered brow. A Navajo blessing rite, or hozoniji, was per-formed by Noni, who sang in her Native tongue. Chad held the baby close to his failing eyes and traced her fan-feathered brow with his shaking hand. He smiled and sighed.

"The Clan continues. Little One, so much rests upon those tiny shoulders. I will be gone from Earth, but I will be with you, when your battles appear before you."

Chad and Noni squabbled over the beautiful baby, and stroked the soft, feathery eyebrows that fanned above her luminous, new-blue eyes. Her Egyptian name, Sesheta, was the name of the Egyptian goddess of history, for this baby would make and keep the history of her clan, someday. Noni gave her the Navajo middle name Tsilkali, meaning "Little Bird," for Noni affectionately foretold that this "brave little bird will find the pollen for her people." (Pollen is the Navajo symbol for peace.) Her two year-old brother, Collin, could only pronounce his own name for her: Pepper. From infancy, then, the child named for an Egyptian goddess and a Navajo prophecy became known only as Pepper.

The baby was active from the start, and kept her extended family in a state of exhaustion. Alaiya nursed and cooed to this baby as she had with Collin, but something made her wary of losing herself in love to this child of prophecy.

Purification Countdown was a massive undertaking, and Jim was often in the underground palaces with Alaiya's mother and the other scientist engineers. Rahd spoke desperately to the world, on televi-sion and in Congress, explaining the impending doom, and Earth people's need to change the pattern of the comet with concentrated thoughts and hearts and feelings and souls. He was far too distracted and tired to lend much comfort to Alaiya during her time of need. Not only did much of the world laugh at Rahd's efforts to warn peo-ple, but his beloved father—Pepper's Grandfather Chad—was clearly dying. Alaiya's adopted brother, Chris, sat with her while she cried.

Alaiya cried for the end of life as they'd known it during their idyllic youth in the mountains. She cried for the destruction she knew would erupt: the shredded trees, the dead animals, the poisoned air and water. She cried for Collin and Pepper, babies she loved more than life, having to grow up in caves underground, not seeing the sun for years. Chris, the brother of her heart, listened and cried with her.

The day came when the family assembled in the glass and wood mountaintop home in New Mexico, to watch sunset colors whip about them from outside, as they always had, and to say goodbye to Grandfather Chad. Death was an eerie and unfamiliar addition to this achingly familiar routine of sunset colors exploding outside, and ricocheting off the glass windows. Noni sang a terribly sad song in her language that sent shivers through Alaiya's lactating body. She was grateful to be nursing Baby Pepper and holding little Collin on her lap. These babies were her body's, as well as her spirit's, comfort.

Noni told the family she would not return with them to the Sierras. "My time will closely follow his," she whispered. In the ancient way, she knew her time was coming, "to join with the wind and my man."

Collin and Pepper seemed to sense an excitement that was dark in the air. Others versed in the Ancient Ways would later talk about the babes that were born just before the Purification, and how different they were from babes that came before. Collin was watchful and wise, and not much like a child. Pepper was more like a baby, but Alaiya would find herself getting lost in the baby's eyes, which had turned as deep a golden green as her own. Long, ancient stories lived in those eyes, and the baby stared up at her patiently, as if trying to tell Alaiya the stories.

2010 was the year the science community planned to go underground. Not all scientists believed the comet would harm Earth; they reminded world leaders of the early days, back in 2002, when a comet the size of ten football fields splashed harmlessly into the Indian Ocean.

Alaiya would remember 2009 as a surreal time: raising a toddler, nursing one baby, and then, accidentally, finding herself pregnant with another. During this remarkable insistence by her body to continue her race, she helped bury her beloved Noni, who died in the early days of '09. With her parents and Jim, she planned her family's move to the caves.

Most of the others were settled in their new homes underground while Alaiya and Jim waited above for their third child to come. Sandy was working below, overseeing all operations. Chris was acting as nanny to Collin and Pepper when Alaiya's contractions began.

Considering the tremendous stress of their lives since discovering the path of the comet, Alaiya's third baby was born easily, in April of 2010. She checked for the fan-feathered brow on this new boy, and saw only the faintest, baby-hint of a normal brow. The baby giggled up at her, as if to assure her he would be easy, an asset in the travails to come. She inhaled the rich fragrance of his scalp, and called him Sol, the Spanish word for sun. Saying his name would give them all hope of seeing the sun again, someday.

The planet looked magically enduring and green on the day in May Alaiya, Jim, Chris, and the three children spent their last day above ground. The day was long, and Alaiya pleaded with her adoring husband to wait until twilight's colors had completely faded from the sky before he let her take them below. In a ceremony she'd learned from her Navajo grandmother, Alaiya kissed the sand on the shores of Lake Tahoe. She took a handful of earth for each of them, and put the earth into pouches her grandmother had given her before she died.

"Here, each of you take one," she ordered. "Taking this earth means you will return, someday."

When she shoved an earth-filled pouch into little Pepper's two-year-old hand, Pepper brought the pouch to her heart and smiled deeply at her mother. "It'll be okay, Mommy," Pepper said.

Alaiya's silent tears fell, and the family went to the cable car that would take them two miles below the earth. They rode the car deep into the darkness. This was the final car, and when they were inside the heavy, iron door, the door slammed shut with a huge, final bang.

Sandy and Rahd were on the landing as the cable car opened. Collin ran to his beloved grandfather, and Rahd lifted him with love. Alaiya and Jim blinked at the world they would call home for several years. It was a lovely city, full of light, and hewn into the deep rock foundation of Earth. Greenery flourished everywhere, filling the city with life-giving oxygen. Really, it was like a brightly lit jungle! Small, one-story adobe buildings were practically hidden behind trees and foliage.

Jim stroked Alaiya's arm. "Scientists determined which rain forest botanicals give off the most oxygen, and we filled our world with them."

The humid air reminded all of them of Florida. Pepper and Collin ran off with "Uncle Chris" to play in a swimming pool their grandparents were telling them about, leaving Jim and Alaiya and tiny Sol to spend some time touring their new home. Two hundred scientists and their families would live in this self-contained jungle, until the probes above—well monitored from the computer station below—told them the comet's ash and toxic air and water had been cleansed by time.

The Earth Core Tunnels consisted of a maze with small adobe huts for each family unit. A constant whir from the engines circulated oxygen all through the "palaces" and tunnels.

Jim was excited about the ingenuity of the place, and Alaiya felt infected by his excitement. He took her to the food-growing area, and she gasped at the vastness of it. They visited the "park," where a football-sized field covered in clover grew, with a jungle gym and a swimming pool to the side of the field.

"The pool is constantly churning, and is lined in copper, so the water will stay clean. It'll be like swimming upstream," he said. "It was my idea—for you. I thought you'd be happier if you had a pool."

Alaiya's eyes grew full as she looked at this man who'd loved her with everything he had, for so many years. "Thank you," was all she could say.

"There's so much to show you. First, look up."

Alaiya looked up, and gasped. There was a perfect night sky, with stars above them, exactly where the stars were in the outer world, above Lake Tahoe. "So beautiful!" she said.

"Whenever positions change outside, they'll change here. We'll even see a reproduction of the comet as it approaches Earth, but, of course, our comet down here will only be a hologram."

"Incredible!" Alaiya said.

"C'mon," Jim said, taking Sol from her arms. They wandered through a lush maze of jungle greenery until they came to a room filled with machines. "The Sunset Room!" Jim shouted. They went into the room filled with machines, and she laughed.

"There will be a sunset every evening, and a sunrise every morning, exactly coinciding with the ones outside. It will rain here, probably a lot, with all the humidity, and we'll collect the water in giant cisterns everywhere."

"Fantastic, Jim. You've been busy!"

His face grew solemn. He took Alaiya by the shoulders, and said, seriously, "We're going to make the best of this. We're all going to learn, and grow, and if this crazy plan works, we'll survive a massive catastrophe to make a better world when we go back up."

He took Alaiya and the baby to the library, a two story, huge adobe building filled with floor-to-ceiling shelves of books. There were also computers, Jim told her, whose hard drives were filled with millions more books.

Sol began to wail. It was time to feed the tiny infant and go to their new home for their first night underground. Jim walked her through another lush, green maze to their home. It was simple, with an earthen floor, and plants were everywhere. There was no glass on any of the windows. They lay the baby in a tiny crib, and went into Pepper's and Collin's room to kiss them goodnight. Jim had told Alaiya the temperature would stay constant—a balmy 80 degrees Fahrenheidt—so food growing would be easy. They'd never need blankets, or jackets. For only a moment, Alaiya mourned the loss of sweet, pure, mountain snow.

"Mommy, it will be fun, living here," Collin said drowsily as he went to sleep.

Pepper, sound asleep on her little cot, wore a smile on her beautiful baby face. Alaiya felt like a girl, saying goodnight to her parents, whom she hadn't lived with since before college. She fell into a dark chasm of the deepest sleep.

Life underground was joyful for the Browne-McCullah family. Everyone in the underground community had many tasks to perform each day in order to keep things running smoothly. It was hard work, but there seemed to be more time for play than there'd been above. The community was close, and evenings often found them singing together, or playing charades. There was always a wonderful lecture to listen to in the library, and on a stage in the park, actors would perform plays. Sometimes, on their movie screen, they would watch movies or TV series they had saved on CD's before descending to the Earth Core Tunnels. (Pepper never tired of watching old *Xena, Warrior Princess* episodes.) Alaiya felt she were on a vacation; this place felt like Disneyworld!

Alaiya McCullah would always remember the first time Jim pulled out his football. It was the last football he'd ever thrown, in a clutch performance that would have sent them to the playoffs if his receiver hadn't dropped it. She smiled when she saw he'd brought it below.

He and Chris took Collin and Pepper to the field, and Chris and Jim started to play catch. Collin showed no interest, and ran to the jungle gym to play. Pepper, however, was transfixed. She studied the ball as it left her father's hand, and she analyzed Chris' every motion when he caught the ball.

She toddled closer to her father, and held out her hands. Jim looked at his beautiful, two-year-old daughter, with her black curls, and laughed. He gently tossed her a ball, fully expecting her to be a normal two year old, without the hand-eye coordination to catch a football.

Pepper caught the ball adroitly.

"Hey! How about that? I wish you'd been there for that game against the Lions! We'd have made it to the playoffs! Let's see if you can do it again, Pepper."

Pepper caught the ball again, and put the ball on the ground. She put her hands on her hips, and glared at her father, demanding a serious challenge.

"Okay, okay, Boss, I'll move back. See if you can catch this, little Pumpkin," Jim said, and he threw her an impossible catch, very gently.

Pepper caught the ball again.

"Oh, my God!" Jim shouted. Several people in the came running. Jim and Pepper were laughing.

"What's wrong?" Alaiya shrieked, frightening Sol.

"Look at this!" He shouted. By now, many people stood beside Alaiya, watching.

Jim threw the ball again and again, and Pepper caught it. He wanted her to go out for a pass, but she didn't understand.

"Chris! Come here and show Pepper how to go out for a pass!" Jim commanded, and the people in the crowd looked at Alaiya dubiously.

Chris told Pepper to watch, and she did. Chris exaggerated his movements as he went out for a pass, and caught the ball, pulling it into his chest.

Pepper laughed, and mimicked Chris' every move. Jim, on his knees so he'd be close to Pepper's height, gently threw her the ball as she toddled away from him.

Miraculously, Pepper caught that one, too. Everyone in the park, including Alaiya, gasped. Jim grinned widely, and jumped. "I've got a star wide receiver here!" He shouted.

Pepper laughed. "Again, Daddy."

They played that day for hours. Neither Pepper nor her father seemed to tire of the game, which forged Pepper's deep bond with her father. Living two miles beneath the shores of Lake Tahoe, Pepper McCullah developed the football skills that would make her a star when she re-entered the broken world above.

When she wasn't playing catch with her father in the clover at the park, Pepper was learning from her mother. Alaiya became the teacher of the youngest children in the community. They took their lessons in the library, and Pepper showed special interest whenever they learned about Egypt, or the wisdom of the Native Americans.

Alaiya took it upon herself to learn the ancient wisdom her grandfather Chad had told her she must someday learn. She learned of Mu, the ancient Motherland, and Atlantis, in many ways a cultural child of Mu. Many Muan traders, Alaiya learned, had lived in the lush, verdant valleys of Atlantis, "the Red Land". When Mu sank, the Muans—also called Lemurians—living on Atlantis carried forth Mu's wisdom. About three thousand years after Mu's destruction, cataclysm also took Atlantis to the bottom of the ocean floor.

Atlanteans had been a wandering people, however, and legends of Mu's destruction had stayed very much alive. Atlanteans had wandered all over the planet by the time their own, lovely island continent of Atlantis sank, so her wisdom was also preserved, if hidden.

Alaiya learned of the caves deep inside the mountains of Tibet, where stone tablets from Mu were still buried, telling the secrets of mind over matter. Using the computer room, she probed for ancient wisdom in the monastery libraries deep in the Himalayas. Alaiya taught herself invaluable healing skills used by healers in Atlantis: she learned about the magnitude of power once locked within the crystal rocks. Her mother, Sandy, had brought buckets of crystals down to the underground palaces, as if she knew secrets to uncover. It would be Alaiya's determination that would unearth the greatest of the long-lost wonders.

Eons ago, an immeasurably high intelligence was locked inside rock crystals by their own design. Intelligent, spiritual essences of light chose to dwell in these magical, lustrous rocks. The vast wisdom of these spirits' hearts could be wakened, using messages directed into the heart of the stones from the heart of the healer. The stone would only waken, so the legend told, if the healer's heart was true, and the healer's purpose was one of love.

Alaiya not only found these studies fascinating, but somewhere in the deepest part of her, she knew it was real, true, and that her planet's destiny rested in this ancient knowledge. Her ancestors had practiced this healing from the heart, and she determined that, while down here hiding from a giant comet, she would perfect this magic of healing love. The world above would need it when they emerged.

One night, in early December of the year 2012, Alaiya woke in a sweat. She felt the presence of spirits, because the room went chilly all around her. Her Grandmother Noni was there, filling the room with her love, as was Grandfather Chad. They said nothing, but looked at her with complete love. The mother ibis Alaiya had met on the mountaintop in New Mexico was there, as was the great owl, Caleina. The mother ibis stood behind Caleina, with her white wings outstretched.

Caleina appeared to be backlit with tremendous white light radiating from the Mother Ibis. The great owl spoke. "You have prepared your family well, Alaiya," Caleina said. "The great comet is coming, and on December 23rd, as predicted for thousands of years, Earth will be ripped apart."

Tears came to Alaiya's eyes. "Is there nothing we can do to stop it, to save the lives above?"

"No. Billions of animal and human lives above will carpet and fertilize the new earth, and the new ocean floor. Periodic purification has always been the way. My ancestors were dinosaurs, so I know," Caleina said with a smile. "Amazingly, there will be some fierce warriors from above who will survive. Their struggles will harden them. You will approach them gently, with love in your heart, and some will join you. Others will not," she sighed, "and the same damnable human fight between good and evil will begin on the warm ashes of the old wars. Your daughter Sesheta has the power to end all of the struggles with her great lioness of a heart."

"Pepper?" Alaiya asked, her green eyes wide with disbelief. "All she cares about is football."

Caleina's feathers fluttered, and Alaiya was certain she heard laughter that sounded like tiny, tinkling bells. "Pepper's football will take her to the transformation place where her true powers will be ignited," she said. "When it seems the worst has happened to her, you, Alaiya, must be a strong, wise mother. You will know it is only the beginning of the greater good for all. Do not attempt to heal her."

"I'm frightened by all this," Alaiya said to Noni and Chad.

"Just be your True, shining self, Alaiya," her grandparents said to her without speaking. The visions of her grandparents and Caleina and the mother ibis faded.

That midnight visit changed Alaiya's life forever; she now burned with purpose in her lessons. She felt an urgent need to teach her daughter the history of the Clan of the Fan-Feathered Brow. Pepper seemed to pay no attention during these lessons. Alaiya sighed often, and sometimes slammed her books closed in frustration, but she trusted the midnight vision. She studied the books from the past in earnest, after sending Pepper outside to play football with her uncle and her father. Sending the child away kept Alaiya from losing her temper.

Earth Core Tunnel legend says that one of Alaiya's child students was climbing the bookshelves of the giant library when he fell from a terrible height, breaking his spine. He was paralyzed, but Alaiya, it is said, went to the child and calmly told him he was completely healed. Murmuring those words—"you are completely healed,"—she passed a glowing, clear crystal back and forth across his body. The other children say Alaiya's hands emanated light, and she directed the light at the boy. When she told him to rise, he did. He was completely healed.

Alaiya became the Mother of the Earth Core Tunnel Palace Dwellers. She was not a doctor, and yet people came to her when they needed healing: when their stomachs were upset, or their hearts were troubled, Alaiya always gave them comfort and healed them with a light that emanated from her hands and her heart. Her heart grew larger and wiser as she studied the crystals within the stone. They spoke to her about loving, life, and healing.

Alaiya and Pepper would not forge their destiny's bond until years after they'd emerged back into the world above. An accident would snap Pepper's spine in two. The moment it would happen, Alaiya would know immediately that this was the meaning of that midnight visit in the Earth Core Tunnels. Alaiya would know in the marrow of her bones, this snapping of Pepper's spine was to open her daughter's body, heart, and spirit to the healing ways of the universe. It would take every ounce of her strength not to respond as a mother and instantly heal her daughter's spine. Her husband would glare at her to heal Pepper, and a temporary rift between them would form. Her desire to heal Pepper would drive her nearly mad, but a much bigger destiny demanded she did not.

Until such events transpired, Pepper would remain "Daddy's girl." Collin and Chris and Jim worshipped Pepper, and Pepper wore their worship like a beautiful mane. She shook this mane of worship sauc-ily about her shoulders, and bounced with graceful energy when she walked. She was loved, and how greatly she loved being loved! Sol—a quiet baby who rarely ventured outside Alaiya's arms—was Alaiya's fragrant, constant link to the here and now of life. They made a happy family; everyone had a place of comfort, but wherever they were, each felt surrounded with love.

Alaiya had noticed a pale, quiet young woman, Jenny, following her brother wherever he went. Chris finally noticed her, and a beau-tiful love blossomed. Chris and Jenny's wedding was the first per-formed in the underground palace chambers. The adobe chapel, surrounded with lush, jungle plants, was decorated with tropical flowers for the occasion: gardenias, lotus flowers, and red, pink, and honey-colored hibiscus. Jenny wore a gardenia behind one ear; the lovely wedding gave everyone the gift of hope. Although she missed the sun and mountains, Alaiya had to admit it: their life under-ground was happy.

The scientists all gathered in the monitoring station to watch what they could of the giant comet's destruction of Earth, on December 23, 2012, exactly as the Mayans, Hopi, Egyptians, and others had predicted. Two miles below the earth's surface, incredibly, only a mild quaking shook the tunnels. Above them, however, the destruc-tion was way beyond the worst of their calculations. The community down below held prayer sessions daily, praying for all the ones above who had died. There was terrible sorrow and weeping for days, and, predictably, most of the cameras above were smashed to bits in the cataclysm.

All was now dark above; the sun's rays were completely blocked from reaching Earth's surface. The only way to monitor the destruc-tion above was an ingenious, sonic calculator. This calculator mirac-ulously survived the cataclysm, and lay flat upon the wasted ground, sending sonar signals that told the scientist about acid levels in the rain and air above. The sounds emitting from the sonic device sent the scientists a chemical code. The code told them an all-consuming fire raged throughout the planet, sending layers and layers of ash into the atmosphere that blocked out all sunlight.

After a solid month of mourning, praying, and weeping, however, the scientific community dwelling in the Earth Core Tunnels' palace chambers decided to return to their peacefully productive way of life. Animals and plants multiplied, food grew, and waste was recycled. Children laughed and played and learned and flourished.

Alaiya's mother, Sandy, one of the premier elite scientists of the community, labored many hours with other scientists in the library, every day. They studied the comets of the past, especially the one millions of years ago, made famous for ending the dinosaur's reign on Earth. The pattern of fire and ash and darkness and cold was exactly the same as this new comet's route seemed to be taking. Sandy and the others studied hard, trying to figure what course Earth and the heavens would take, once the cycle of destruction ended and the new one of regeneration began.

While Sandy and the scientists labored in the library, Rahd and his daughter, Alaiya, labored on the planet's spiritual future, based on the most ancient past. They read the works of the mystics, from Zoastrians in Persia, to the Tibetans in the Himalayas. They read the Toltec and the Sioux and the Apaches' detailed descriptions of their ancestors who came from "The Red Land"—Atlantis. All of them had similar, mystical traditions that could be accessed by learning various ways of breathing, and going deep inside the self.

This, of course, had been Rahd's life's work, as it had been his parents' life's work. He was determined to find the mystical link that would unite all the ancient, mystical traditions that seemed to scatter about the planet when Atlantis sank. Pockets of her great spiritual culture existed on every continent, for the Atlanteans had been great travelers. If the planet were to survive, however, all the pockets would have to be woven into one cohesive fabric of ultimate wisdom: heart and mind over matter, or, love conquering all.

In May of 2014, the sonic monitors' beeps suggested to all the scientists in all the Earth Core Tunnel palace chambers all over the world that human life might again be supported above ground. One brave scientist would have to volunteer to go above with vials to test the air and water. Jim volunteered, infuriating Alaiya and Chris.

"How can you do this? You have three kids who need you! Let me go!" Chris demanded.

"Chris, I am the scientist, here, and you and Jenny have a baby on the way. I'm doing this, okay?"

Alaiya recovered from her brief anger long enough to kiss her husband before he rode the cable car to the top. "Come home to me, and to your children," she said.

Jim's stomach churned, and his hands shook with fear as he rode the cable car upward for two miles. The top was opened from a switch below, and when he stepped out, wearing a complete suit and helmet, his crying fogged the bubble of his helmet.

Earth was ruined. He landed in what was once a forest, and now was nothing but barren land covered deeply in ash. He walked to an area he remembered four years ago as a lovely, residential neighborhood. He saw only black, ravaged land covered with maybe four feet of ash.

Through his tears, he saw no life of any kind, yet he continued placing one heavy, sad foot in front of the other. All of a sudden, a tiny bit of green flashed before him. Smaller than the tip of his baby finger, a tiny, green shoot of some kind of houseplant lay on the ground, and on that tiny, green shoot, a ladybug wandered.

How magical this life seemed! The little bug wandered as if she were doing something ordinary, yet she was a great miracle. Jim shouted inside his helmet; then he took off his helmet to shout and cry again.

"Life! Life!" He lifted the tiny bug onto his finger, and she began to crawl happily about his hand. "I will call you 'Phoenix,' after the lone Egyptian bird who rose from the ashes of death, just as you have."

Pepper McCullah was six years old when the community of scientists and their families rode the cable cars up the long tunnel for two miles, to begin a new life on their scorched planet. For weeks, Pepper had watched the cable cars ride upward, with trees and plants and animals. Now, her mother and father told her, they were moving to a life above. They said it would be hard at first, but then their life would be beautiful, living in the richness of sunshine. Pepper had no idea what sunshine was, but they made it sound wonderful and magical.

The beautiful little girl with black hair, green eyes, and eyebrows that fanned like feathers above her lustrous eyes, carried a football under one arm. With her other hand, she held her father's hand tightly. Her mother watched her carefully, remembering the midnight visit from the spirits of her Clan.

This child is fearless, Alaiya thought. The destiny of many millennia—the destiny of our Clan—awaits us, and lies in the tiny hand and lioness heart of a six-year-old girl.

Alaiya, a mother to so many for four years underground, shrieked in horror when she saw her beloved Earth. Black, burnt ground was all there seemed to be. The chilly, Sierra mountain air felt good, nevertheless, and filled her with resolve. With her four-year-old son, Sol, resting on her hip, she climbed a rise, and looked out over the black, barren earth to find a shining blue miracle: Lake Tahoe somehow still existed, and it was still blue! Her entire heart opened, and widened. They'd be all right. She knew it.

All over the planet, scenes such as this were being enacted: underground chambers in what had been Ireland, Tibet, the Yucatan, Arizona, and several other places burst open. They carried their plants and animals to the surface, to rebuild a life on Earth.

On each surviving continent, in tunnel palaces far below the surface of Earth, the ancient ways of living from the heart had been studied hard. The humans rising to the surface after the cataclysm made up a much wiser race than the ones who'd gone below. Their time spent below had given them a space to study, to think, to heal, and to grow in their hearts. Going into the Earth's belly had taught them to know the core of the very heart, and pulse, of life on Earth.

The re-emergence was brutally hard, and the work required to put what was left of the planet back together seemed impossible. But the human race is an indomitable one. They sifted through their old lives to see very clearly what was necessary and what was not, and the rebuilding began.

The Sierra group of scientists, which included the Clan of the Fan-Feathered Brow, first heard of the New Earth Survivors on a sunny day in June. They'd brought battery-powered cell phones from below, and a call came from one of the scientists who'd lived with them in their community for the four years below.

"Jim!" the voice shouted from the other end, "all the underground chamber groups all over the world are finding some people alive, who lived above and survived the whole thing. They climbed down into the Pentagon basement, and the Nebraska warhead hideout, and hurricane cellars. It's like these war places saved lives! Religious types built basements and ransacked grocery stores before the fires ate up everything—we've got some unbelievable survivalist stories! I have to say, though, they're a little skittish. They could use Alaiya's TLC, let me tell you!"

And so, the Earth Core Tunnel people met the New Earth People. Alaiya embraced many ragged, New Earth survivors, and both groups began to work together to rebuild their planet and their lives. Each had valuable survival techniques to share.

Before the cataclysm, the earth had held about seven billion people on her seven continents. Six billion people had perished in the explosion and subsequent fires, in the largest cataclysm ever faced by this earth and her inhabitants. The one billion remaining felt determined to use this glorious second chance. (Well, it was *their* second chance, as Earth had been purged many times before in cataclysms, as many stone tablets from Mu, Atlantis, and the Bible had attested). They would build life of freedom, love, and joy. They felt their salvation was a sign from God, as in olden, Biblical days; they were the chosen people. They hoped to get it right this time, and create an earth where all people were equal, and felt loved.

A few schools began rising, like the mythical, Egyptian phoenix from the blackened earth. Alaiya and Jim's alma mater, Stanford University, was now at the bottom of the sea, along with the rest of the California coast. The satiated ocean now lapped at the once-red earth of Placerville, California, so from the ash-blackened shores of Placerville, the new Stanford University began to rise.

With precious, functional machines collected from Earth Core Tunnels all over the world, books and wisdom were shared and duplicated. New and old energy sources, using the wisdom from the underground chambers, created clean-burning energy to fuel the rebuilding of a civilization.

The children who'd lived in the Earth Core Tunnels throughout the world had spent their time learning at an accelerated pace. When Pepper was twelve, in 2020, she was ready to begin high school. Her high school, Hope High, was a tiny group of ash adobe huts, powered by methane and clean-burning coal. Wise, gentle survivors of the great cataclysm took turns teaching. It was Pepper and her father—a dedicated teacher at the school—who filled the school with enthusiasm about football.

It amuses the Sea Faeries when I teach them about the culture of the humans. After the incredibly vast destruction of Earth, the Sea Faeries think it precious that the Earth humans chose to restore their games: hockey and football, baseball and basketball. I compare it with our love of games below: if our ocean floor world were destroyed, wouldn't our kingdoms work day and night to repair the Sea Cricket Domed Palace?

In 2024, Pepper was ready to enter Stanford University, at the age of sixteen. The ash adobe huts on the coast in Placerville blended well with the ash-blackened earth around them. Upon emerging from the Earth Core tunnels, scientists in 2014 had planted quick-growing, magically germinating trees genetically engineered to seek nourishment from ash. The more desolate, and buried in ash the landscape, the more rapidly these lovely trees grew and germinated. By 2024, they densely covered the ash-blackened earth in Placerville.

As memory keeper, I have closely studied and documented Pepper's rise to football fame, and the accident that snapped her back in 2029. With the faeries and my Queen, I watched as a rebuilt nation filled her broken body with the light of love. It was a glorious moment in human history, watching their good souls pray for her as she lay on the field. We heard their words, "Please get up, Pepper," and we watched her being light up with radiance from their love. We rejoiced, for it meant the time of transformation for the new, purified planet, was at hand.

When the accident happened, it was Alaiya, of all the humans, who knew what the moment meant. While her father, Jim, suffered terrible torment over Pepper's injured spine, Alaiya understood the import of Pepper's broken spine: she would now be able to receive energy directly from the earth's core. Properly trained, Pepper would someday be able to help free the Light Beings who dwelled within the Sun Quartz Fields. Alaiya withstood her husband's angry glares when he demanded she heal Pepper, as she once had healed a boy in the Earth Core Tunnels. Alaiya turned away because it was what she wanted to do more than anything, yet she was bound by the destiny of her clan.

Pepper also waited, at first, for her mother to simply come and "make it better," as she always had in the past, with every conceivable ailment and injury. Puzzled and betrayed when no healing occurred, she accepted Aliaya's explanations of destiny and bore her disappointment. She felt tremendous comfort in her mother's arms, as Alaiya nursed her. A deep bond she'd not yet felt with her mother was forged in those early days after Pepper's accident. Pepper would never know the restraint Alaiya forced upon herself not to use her healing powers to heal Pepper's spine. To focus her energy elsewhere, Alaiya labored to finally make the captive young woman listen to both her history and her destiny. Alaiya was the only person Pepper enjoyed being with, although Pepper was baffled by Alaiya's happiness over Pepper's broken spine. At least her mother was cheerful! Indeed, it was Alaiya who introduced Pepper to the Wisdom Palace, where Alaiya had first served as teacher.

It was Rahd, Alaiya's father, who instinctively knew where to find the magical pink quartz fields deep in space that were suddenly visible in the heavens following Gonaquadet. Alaiya had translated the ancient wisdom texts during her time in the Earth Core tunnels, and Alaiya had told her father of the ancient secrets revealed and cherished by the Clan of the Fan-Feathered brow, down through the millennia.

A space expedition was launched, with Sandy, Alaiya, and Rahd on board. Sandy took the astronauts and other geologists where her husband led them, five million miles into space. They rejoiced when they uncovered acre after acre of the magical, pink fields of space rocks. The Sun Quartz Fields were as big as the planet Venus, and could now easily be seen as a brilliant, flashing pink light in the sky. From space, however, they beckoned and dazzled with their promise.

The Sun Quartz Fields had been created over millions of years, but, because of their great power and vulnerability, the fields had been protected from the view of pre-apocalypse, greedy earthlings. The Kobans and the mighty Zoloatons (enlightened citizens of the planet Zoloat) had united their forces of mind-heart-and-spirit to create a huge invisibility shield around the Sun Quartz Fields. Only now, after Earth people had learned the hard lessons of the heart taught by Gonaquadet, did the joined forces of Koba and Zoloat agree to let Earthlings see and know their power and promise.

Few experts in these matters imagined it a coincidence when, shortly after the discovery of the Sun Quartz Fields, Sandy and her geological team uncovered vast heaps of pink quartz in the magical rock canyons of Arizona. They whooped like soot-covered children at their discovery. Buried beneath mountains of ash, the pink quartz that stretched for miles seemed to be a consolation gift of beauty from Gonaquadet.

Alaiya and Rahd understood exactly what they had seen in space, and what must be done to ready Earth for the awakening of the Sun Quartz Fields. They fought with Sandy over the need to build a Wisdom Palace entirely of this Arizona pink quartz, high in the Sierras. There, they pleaded with Sandy, Wisdom Retrievers would recover all the ancient knowledge necessary to reawaken the light beings slumbering within the Sun Quartz Fields. Sandy, in the end, had to give in to the two people on Earth she loved most.

"Pink quartz is the stone that opens the heart, Mother," Alaiya said softly. "It was meant to be."

The story of the Clan of the Fan-Feathered Brow has woven its circle of stories-within-the-story. We are now, at this writing, in Earth human time, in the year 2030. Pepper is becoming a brilliant Wisdom Retriever. The Winter Solstice is approaching, on December 23—eighteen years after the cataclysmic destruction of much of Earth—at midnight, the Sun Quartz Fields will open their receptors. At that moment, the final battle for Light and Wisdom and Love over Darkness will be waged. We have a few months for the emissaries of the light warrior clans to learn all we have to teach them.

We have one formidable enemy: Tronot, the reincarnation of Memsek. Memsek killed Nanu, mother of the Clan of the Fan-Feathered Brow, and Tronot has already killed people merely for annoying him. Darkness is his only food, and the power of darkness is his only need. He loves money, but money in itself is not evil. He wants complete power over the limitless energy source the Sun Quartz Fields will provide, more than the money. What he doesn't understand is that the Sun Quartz Fields are made up of all-powerful, yet sensitive, delicate Light Beings. If his darkness triumphs, would destroy them, they will return and into the blissful safety of the Sun Quartz Fields for another million years. Earth does not have that million years, and She will die. Events and their outcome are yet to unfold.

As we wait for the final lifting of the veil, I remain yours, my King and my Queen of Koba,

Marla, Sea Faerie Keeper of Memories.

INSIDE THE PALACE OF THE GREED KINGS

From the Earth Memories Archives
Compiled by Marla, Sea Faerie Keeper
Of Memories

My King and Queen had read my extensive text of memories together, sitting side by side, touching hands as they turned the pages. Down through the ages of the Clan of the Fan-Feathered Brow they had traveled together, by reading my words. When finished, they smiled so radiantly at me, a large orb of sun-hot light filled our world. I will never forget that magical moment of light! All my little sins had been forgiven, and I was never more glad to be a Keeper of Memories. After a long moment of radiant light, my King Kanta spoke while his cloud of white hair swam all around his strong, handsome face.

"Extraordinary, Marla. Your work leaves no detail untouched. We knew we had chosen you well, but you have far exceeded our high expectations. You are gifted, my child."

I bowed and humbly thanked my King.

He continued. "Now, you must document the dark side. Your next duties will take you inside the Palace of the Greed Kings, where 'Memsek'—excuse me, but I always think of him, that way—rather it is Tronot, Memsek's reincarnated descendant of darkness, we must watch now. He knows of the Winter Equinox, and we must watch him in his shifted shape, as the great owl, Caleina, has taught us to do."

I gasped, and turned to Rona, the softer of the two Royals. "Rona, it is terrible to watch this dreadful, dark human," I sulked, for I loved so being coddled like a child by her.

Rona's lovely brow furrowed, and she spoke in a stern tone I was not used to. "You must watch and write and digest the entire report, Marla. We know too little of Tronot. Go, my sweet friend, and, as Keeper of Memories, please leave nothing out in your written report."

I learned to be a royal scribe in Egypt, ten thousand years ago, shortly after the migration of Atlanteans to Egypt. This was long before Nanu's time. It was up to me to save the magical, metaphysical ways of Mu and Atlantis, when the floods buried the Sphinx for a time. I wrote then mostly on stone, and my work was long buried by Memsek in the Hall of Records. It is good to be Marla, because I know so well the stories of Earth, firsthand!

I do love being me. Pepper is a very young and new soul, and being young and new has a certain charm in that. I have no lasting memory of being young or new. For that, however, I doubt I'd trade my ancient stories! And Rona does not only love me as a wise, old friend. She depends on me greatly to save this lovely Earth.

I love the writing, the words, and the languages that have changed so greatly, through the millennia. Cuneiform writing was fun, as were the swaying and swirling of Sanskrit symbols. These new, boxy letters are not so lovely as Sanskrit. As I prepare myself to enter the Palace of the Greed Kings, I feel important, but I also shiver with coldness. I will shift my shape into that of a magnificent Earth woman. Why not toy with the tiny seed in Tronot's ancient DNA memory, leftover from the nasty Memsek? I will shape shift into a beautiful woman resembling Nanu, complete with the fan-feathered brow. I believe this will unsettle Tronot tremendously, giving me an advantage. Oh, it is fun to be me!

Tronot lives and works in the truly garish, bright city of Oceanside, Idaho. The sun shines harshly here, glaring off the silver of glass and horrid cars. The people of this town are an odd sort, worshipping their silly cars that cannot move on the crowded streets. They sit in these cars, reading, typing, watching television, and feeling inexplicably superior to those who do not live in their automobiles. (Gad, you'd think they'd have learned from their last civilization!)

I do enjoy the slender palm trees, however. Though not the date palms of my ancient Egypt, they are lovely. They were planted in 2014 because so many palm seedlings were carried above from the Tunnel Palaces, after the cataclysm. These trees had quite a time, mating like mad in the Earth Core Tunnels!

Hard, remembering how to walk on two funny legs. I made sure to design them in my shape shift, so they were as long and brown and lovely as Nanu's once were.

I entered the large, glass building of Omnipotence International, and walked up to the security guards on the ground floor. I watched their eyes as they watched me, and sensed I had done a good job making myself into an attractive Earth woman.

"Mr. Tronot is expecting me," I said in my new Earth voice. I wanted to giggle at myself—as always—when I assume an Earth shape. "The name is Nora Whitely." While the red-faced security guard was calling Mr. Tronot, I exerted extreme telepathic pressure on Mr. Tronot, so he indeed expected me. The security guard nodded without his stiff, red hair moving even a whit, and he walked me through the metal weapons detector. He unlocked the elevator for me to take to Mr. Tronot's office on the top floor.

From the top floor, I could see the ocean, a dazzling blue lit with billions of crystalline sparkles. I gasped to see my beloved home for millennia from this angle! My king and queen were closer now, and I was filled with strength. I felt them all in my heart as I approached Mr. Tronot.

He was in a bit of a daze from my telepathic work on him, but he liked what he saw, nevertheless. His immediate reaction, when the fog of my telepathy lifted, was quick, Earth male happiness at my beautiful Earth form. I wondered if his ancient DNA would remember, but not for long. Tronot-Memsek's DNA definitely remembered Nanu. His face changed; his eager, male, hormone happiness suddenly shifted. His eyes narrowed, and penetrated mine, trying to remember. His face was lit with recognition, longing, and long-ago desire.

"Oh," was all he could say, when his memory passed like a cloud over his present-day brain. The dark eyes in his cloudy head were those of Memsek's for a moment, and I shuddered. Tronot is no prince, but I was relieved when the dark eyes again became the later, less menacing model. Tronot was a slick, tidy man: well-dressed and attractive, his thick dark hair brushed his brow in waves.

I must remember his present-day name and form, I cautioned myself. "Mr. Tronot," I said, smiling, "I've come to talk to you about the Winter Equinox."

"You...look...so...familiar."

"Oooh, you are flirting with an ancient line, Mr. Tronot." My own tongue-in-cheek flirtatiousness was a little nauseating, I confess, but certainly effective.

"No. I mean it! I know I know you from somewhere."

"Egypt, perhaps," I said, allowing a steely flicker to pass into my gaze. I wanted him to cease this patter, so we could get on with my business of saving Earth. My dream of dreams was to become my Koban King and Queen's hero of all the ages.

I do not really enjoy living in the body of an Earth person. The lipstick, the dreadful shoe-things on these ugly feet-things...No. I wanted this business finished, so I could return to my silent, liquid world of peace.

"Egypt," he murmured. "Well, let's get on with the business of the Winter Equinox, when my hundreds of billions will become hundreds of trillions. I will own the Earth's most powerful energy source. Post-cataclysm, hydrogen-fuel-cell powered life will seem just as backward and barbaric as pre-cataclysm, fossil-fuel life seems now. Incredible, isn't it?"

"You will be a very, very powerful man, Mr. Tronot."

"Can I buy you lunch?"

"No." I do not like the Earth people's nasty way of eating, and will avoid it at all costs.

He shifted uncomfortably in his chair. He was still bothered by that nagging, DNA memory. He cleared his throat. "You're all business."

"Yes."

We walked into his inner sanctum, which he opened by using a laser sensor that scanned across his eyes. We entered a massive planetarium. Giant, colorfully painted planets the size of my entire Earth-body hummed as they slowly rotated around the vast sun in the planetarium's distance.

Tronot picked up a large, crystal pointing stick, and pointed its shooting laser to a spot near the golden-red planet, Venus. "Here is your destiny: the Sun Quartz Fields. I have a mock-up of the actual Fields in the next room. You'll need sunglasses."

The next room was the size of one of Pepper's football stadiums. I donned the shades, but they were not powerful enough to shield my eyes from the intense, pinkish-golden light coming from the mountain of quartz in the next room. Its hot, powerful light was nearly blinding, and each chunk of quartz shone flawlessly. The only way to describe the mountain of crystal to my king and queen is: think of a single, bright pink diamond as large as a dolphin, and then add another ten thousand dolphin-sized pink diamonds. Each of these giant pink crystals nested on top of each other. Each crystal shone with a million lights, as bright as the sun on the ocean. I gasped aloud when I saw this mock-up of the Sun Quartz Fields.

I walked hundreds of yards on stupid, human feet, reverently around the mountains of pink and golden quartz trapped in this evil man's realm. I knew I was risking my life to save the magical, limitless wonder this replica represented. I vowed to fight to save the Sun Quartz Fields. For the first time, I understood the passion behind the battle, and this was only a replica!

Ulena, and Lillith, my Lemurian mother, and my Atlantean father, Bromand, and my Kobans, and all the Zoloatons behind us, knew this field of miraculous quartz in the heavens was both the means, and the symbol of the means, to free all Earth humans from suffering, forever. When the Winter Equinox's pivotal moment activated the quartz fields with light from the sun, and torque from Jupiter's largest moon, Ganymede, Earth would enter into an era of peace, harmony, and joy. Rather than allow Tronot, this ancient, evil force to take over a massive jewel that could only have been created by God, I, too, would join the Forces of Light to see that the era of perfect joy and love—predicted in every ancient text, in every ancient culture—reigned at last.

"So beautiful," I said quietly. I did not want this man to know my fierce, inner resolve, or do anything that might in any way hint at such resolve.

Tronot considered the Sun Quartz Fields only in profit potential terms, so he shook his black hair and shuffled me into a business mode. His voice grew brisk. "Now. Your records from NASA are fantastic. You trained hard, and became one of their finest astronauts ever. Why did you choose to work for me instead?"

"You're paying more."

"Yes, but you recognize you will become a criminal, and will never work for NASA again."

"I adore the art of spacecraft flight, Mr. Tronot. All I ask for is vast amounts of money, and the opportunity to visit the Sun Quartz Fields often."

"Okay. You will command the lead ship, and there will be five of my ships behind you, following your orders and mine. You understand there will be only brief moments for the six ships to hook up the receptors to drain the fields of their power, so you must move swiftly, and in perfect coordination with the other ships."

"I do understand."

"Good girl."

"I'm not a girl, Mr. Tronot."

"Of course not. My apologies." His dark eyes scanned my fan-feathered brow. He paused, looking for something to say. "You remind me of someone I knew as a little girl."

"I understand." I smiled slyly. He had no idea how much I knew!

"Let's talk about our allies and our enemies. Our allies are, of course, all the power companies. They are willing to allow me the honor, not to mention the multi-billion dollar expense, to do the hook-up. They understand I get first cash, of course, although I am going to sell subdivided plots of the fields to the highest bidders."

"Great. Our enemies?" Did he notice the hostile curl of my human lip, or the sarcastic tone in my voice?

"Oh, those poopy little psycho faeries in the Wisdom Palace, who have a friend in our ridiculous White House. I plan to nuke that whole damned establishment."

"You're going to nuke Lake Tahoe and the Wisdom Palace?" I took a gulp of air, trying to remain calm.

He noticed my alarm, and smiled a greasy smile at me. "You think it's a bad idea? There are other lakes."

"It's a very bad idea, Sir. Lake Tahoe is a global treasure."

His smile grew greasier. "That Wisdom Palace is worse than a nuisance to those of us who believe it is our inalienable right to use the resources God gave us in order to profit."

It took millennia worth of Ascension training for me to refrain myself from smacking this man across the room. How do Earth peo-

ple get this way, where all they want is money, and ridiculous posses-
sions?

"If you destroy the western United States so it is unfit for human
habitation, you will lose countless billions in energy revenues," I
said.

"Maybe you're right. But those goofheads in the Palace possess
powers I have no way to acquire. That makes them dangerous."

Inside my head, I was smiling. Dark little human, you have no
idea how very, very backward you are. How do humans go backward,
this way? I've watched it again and again, down through the millennia. It always amazes me. Theirs is a world without spirit; a foolish
world of concrete stuff.

To Tronot's face, I lied. "Mr. Tronot, I have been inside the Wisdom Palace, and I can assure you, the powers of the 'psycho fairies,'
as you refer to them, are absolutely nothing compared with your
powers."

Predictably, he cherished my lie, and swallowed it whole. I've met
the Wise Ones, the ones who live a life based in the heart and the
soul. They are filled with joy, and love. Having met them, I wonder
why dark people like Tronot, so obsessed with the Material World,
still exist. Why have they not gone the way of the dinosaur—extinct
on this earth, and whisked off to Dimension Eight, where they won't
be so destructive? I knew the answer, of course. Tronot's destiny is to
save Earth. This legend had been learned, but it was hard to digest, as
I stood there, that day.

Tronot led me back to the security guards downstairs. He took my
hand into his clammy one, which reminded me of a tentacle.

"It will be fantastic, working together," he promised, kissing my
human hand.

"Absolutely," I said, smiling. I left, and then traveled with magical
sea faerie swiftness past the lovely coast with its palms and cliffs.
Whirling about in the sea faerie way, I returned to my favorite form.
I splashed into the water, and was eagerly greeted by some of my dol-

phin friends. Surging below the sea in my true, free form was heaven. The dolphins teased me about the human shape I'd worn with Tronot, but I only laughed.

"Rona is a hard queen, indeed, making me do this horrible work to save these silly humans," I laughed in a dolphin's face. "Why am I even apologizing to you? You love the humans more than I do, you little hypocrites."

The dolphins laughed, as they always do. Laughter is their prayer, their constant way of blessing all things: things of this world, and of all worlds. Echoes of their joyous laughter can be heard even in space, among the cosmos. Dolphin laughter is considered sacred, up there, and all planets' beings cherish it. This is why the meteor Gonaquadet could not wipe out the dolphins as a species. In our faerie tales for faerie children in the River of Life, it is written that one dolphin laughed, and her laughter whirled up in the air before her, spawning a loving mate who gave her many children. I still believe it, although I know what also happened. Just before Gonaquadet exploded, the dolphins and whales and fishes and sea creatures were magically swept into another dimension by the Prime Creator, Earth humans' God. While havoc ruled Earth, creatures of the sea were for a time reunited with the dinosaurs, in dimension Eight.

Perhaps I will someday live as a dolphin, for a time. A playful Sea Faerie could certainly enjoy herself as a dolphin! I will think about asking my King and Queen when my job with Earth is done. I will need some playtime!

I must talk to Rona about what I have learned in the Greed Kings' palace, and then I will meet with Ulena, so everyone may strategize. The battle will be fierce. Thankfully, strategy is not my problem. I am only the Sea Faerie Keeper of Memories, down through the ages. The scribe. I went to visit Tronot as my duty, and so I could jot down my experiences, as Scribe Royale for my Queen and King.

However, I am changed. I have seen the magical replica of the Sun Quartz Fields. In this magnificent field lies the end of suffering for all the people of Earth, and I am profoundly moved by it. It was only a replica, yet a very good one, and I sensed the immense power and love emanating from the Light Beings dwelling within the fields. If all goes well, at the right moment, their huge, all-encompassing love will explode into the cosmos like fireworks, and this universe will be transformed. One dark little man and his legions cannot destroy that. I will gladly give my life to defeat Evil and Darkness.

STRATEGIES ARE DISCUSSED

From the Earth Memories Archives
Compiled by Marla, Sea Faerie Keeper
Of Memories

Ulena, Queen Rona, and King Kanta sat with Sandy, Rahd, and their daughter, Alaiya, in a beautiful room in the Koba Palace, far below the sea in the River of Life. I was there, too, acting as the observer, informer, and scribe. I sat up a little taller, plumping myself happily among neon-pink, cabbage-sized sea roses Rona had set all around us. I had gathered Pepper McCullah's scientist parents and grandparents to explain to my King and Queen exactly how the Sun Quartz Fields would be awakened and protected.

I began by directing my questions to Alaiya. "Alaiya, it was you who discovered the Sun Quartz Fields. Please tell my King and Queen how certain you are of their potential for activation at midnight of the 23rd."

Alaiya spoke to all of us, turning her pretty, chestnut head of hair this way and that. "Certainly. The Light Beings within the crystals will come alive, as if waking from a long, deep sleep. The Sun Quartz Fields are out in space, about five million miles from here, and about three million miles from Venus. Energy from the sun, and massive torque from Ganymede—Jupiter's biggest moon—will ignite the fields' physical energy at the exact moment of Equinox. It will be an unforgettable event to witness, even here on Earth."

Aliaya paused, beaming with joy. With her sparkling, green-gold eyes, she reminded me of her exuberant daughter, Pepper. "With recovery of ancient knowledge of the language and music the Light Beings once used to communicate, the Wisdom Retrievers will be able to speak to them of our wishes. With their light and profound knowledge and love, the Light Beings will herald a new age of harmony in the universe, with the massive energy emanating from the Sun Quartz Fields."

King Kanta's face, so often purple from all the toxins he'd once digested to save the seas, brightened to a gentle lavender. He listened to Alaiya's promise of the joys to come. His face, always strong, softened; it was a beautiful face. "Marla?" King Kanta asked, turning to me.

I fidgeted, feeling shy. "Tronot has complete understanding of the Sun Quartz Fields' *physical* awakening," I said, "and he has several ships that will be waiting for the precise moment, with massive hoses and equipment to harness and contain the energy. I have signed on as his astronaut and scientific expert."

"But if he succeeds," Alaiya rudely interrupted me, "the crystal fields will very quickly return to their inanimate state! They will wither, and return to their sleep of bliss for at least another million years! Marla, blissful or not, the Light Beings have not slept all these eons in order to be chained and harnessed by forces of darkness. They won't do it! Everything will be lost." She smashed her fist on the table, upsetting a Sea Rose.

"No!" I gasped. I could not bear it. The possibility was too horrible. The Light Beings had waited eons to be activated, and their activation was crucial to Earth. My King and Queen and I, along with the other Ascended Masters in the River of Life, had also waited millennia for this magical event.

My beautiful Queen Rona put her hand gently on mine to soothe me. "Marla, failure is neither an option nor a possibility, here. Alaiya, how do you feel the progress with the warriors from the Light Clans is going?"

"Very well, Queen Rona. They are quick, eager, motivated students."

"And your daughter? We chose her well, did we not?"

Alaiya's wide smile lit the room. "I am very proud of her. She doubts herself, but, as you well know from the ancient Wisdom texts, the human moment of deepest insecurity is the most powerful springboard from which to leap. When she is faced with the actual face-to-face combat with Tronot, she will be true to her deepest self. When her heart binds with the representatives of the other Clans of Light in order to ignite the Sun Quartz Fields, the heavens will explode with their united light."

"Does she understand the danger?" Queen Rona asked.

Alaiya's face fell toward her chest. "Yes, as I do," she answered sadly.

King Kanta wanted spacecraft details, and turned to Sandy. "Sandy, five of the six Clans of Light representatives will be in one of our ships. Pepper and Marla will be in one of Tronot's six ships. We will have two other ships, correct?"

"Yes," Sandy said. She wore glasses, and looked like Caleina. "One ship will be manned by me and my astronauts, and one of them will be manned by Freta and Lars Grenden. They are astronauts from the Clan of the Frozen Fields. Todd is their son, and he'll be in the Clans of Light's ship. All three of our ships will have a Zoloaton on board—they are the finest astronauts in the universe—and the Zoloatons will keep all three ships invisible. Butara the Zoloat will ride with Marla and Pepper."

"Good," King Kanta said simply. He then wanted details on the others from the Clans of Light, and he turned to Ulena. "The six representatives of the Clans of Light will all be in space, at the actual fields during activation. Do they each understand exactly what their role is?"

Ulena smiled, and beamed with pride. Sleek and silver-eyed, with her long, graceful neck, she was like a graceful mother swan clucking proudly about her chicks. "Oh, yes, King Kanta! Their training has gone better than I'd dreamed, thanks to the Zoloatons' help. Todd, from the Clan of the Frozen Fields, is learning to unlock the language of the runes. He will sing the chants of the runes, while Danu of the Forest Clan plays the ancient music the Light Beings once loved. Her music and Todd's runes will awaken the Light Beings. Arinne of the Clan Beyond the Mists knows the ancient legends and prayers the Light Beings once fell asleep to, as babes a million years ago. She will sing them in their ancient language. Tamdin, of the Clan of the Highest Peaks, and Micah of the Clan of Rock and Sun—they are both experts at talking to the Light Beings that dwell in the minerals of rocks here on Earth. They will explain to the Light Beings how Earth's children have relearned the ancient lessons. They will plead for Earth, saying we are finally ready to live without suffering, in complete harmony. Then they will transmit the Light Beings' feelings to all of us. I could not be happier with the Clans of Light, and their Wisdom progress."

Kanta was impatient and gruff. "What about the other twelve athletes, the ones who will stay in the Palace? How goes their Wisdom Training?"

Ulena smiled brightly again before fixing her lovely blind eyes in King Kanta's direction. It was clear Ulena loved her students, with all her heart. "Each one of them is like a pod of light. With their broken spines open to the ley lines, or vortex cracks in the Earth which lead to Earth's energetic core, the twelve of them have been training to work together as a powerful force to receive the activated energy from the Sun Quartz Fields. Their bodies and minds and hearts and souls will unite, to transmit the mighty forces of the fields and the Light Beings, directly into the belly of Earth. Once the energy has penetrated into Earth's core, it will surge upward, through the warriors' bodies. The energy will then shoot the almighty forces of light and harmony all around Earth's circumference."

"Can their bodies sustain that kind of energetic force?"

Ulena's face clouded with sadness. "Maybe not. I cannot promise the warriors will not suffer, or perhaps even die during the transmission of that kind of energetic force that will surge through their open spines. But they understand the risk, and they embrace their roles proudly." She paused for emphasis. "I felt it was important to tell them they may die saving Earth, and they could absolutely quit without shame. Not one of them has quit."

Kanta's face erupted into a vast, kingly smile. It was a gift to us all. He slapped his two large flippers on the table with joy. "Good work, Ulena!" shouted Kanta forcefully. "Let's get on with our mission, then, everyone!"

I CANNOT DO THIS

From the Earth Memories Archives
Compiled by Pepper McCullah
Clan of the Fan-Feathered Brow
Earth year 2030

I sat in my room alone. Thankfully, my brothers and my parents were out. My need to be the cheerful cripple was so intense, around here! It hurt them too much if I broke down, so I couldn't cry without hurting them. I only felt free to cry when they were gone from the house.

I was so down on myself! After hearing about Ulena getting blinded in the Greed Kings' Torture Chamber, and watching Nanu's horribly sad life go by me, I realized what I had to do. I was not made of the heroic stuff these people were. My parents, and grandparents, and all my ancestors in the Clan of the Fan-Feathered Brow—they were all incredibly heroic. The rebuilders of Earth were heroic, during Re-emergence. I was just a crippled football player, witnessing gigantic heroes who talked to me as if I were one of them. It was crazy!

"I am no way as brave or heroic as any of these people! The line of the Clan must've weakened when it got to me," I said, with tears running down my face. As much as I hated to let them all down, my failure was not an option, come Winter Equinox. The stakes were too high to trust a young woman who could never pull it off. Crying while I wrote, I had to write Ulena a letter, resigning.

Dear Ulena,

I wish for you to withdraw my name from your list of Wheelchair Warriors. I cannot do this. I am just a jock. I am an athlete who is not equipped to save anybody from anything. I am way too flawed: I get jealous, I get angry—in fact, I have fits of anger, and depression—and I am too little for this big job.

When I watched all that happened to Nanu in her life, and how unbelievably brave she was, I realized you have picked the wrong person in me. Honestly, Ulena, if I'd been in Nanu's position, I would've given Memsek anything he wanted. I would not have let the flock of ibis take my baby, the way they flew off with little Epu. I would've run away from the Hall of Records with him, before the ibis could ever catch up with him! I wouldn't have been big enough, or brave enough, to care two hoots if the whole world's wisdom secrets were given to the Greed Kings, six thousand years ago! I would just want a happy little life with my chubby little boy. I am not a hero. I am just a girl who wasn't a good enough football player to keep from getting injured. It wasn't just any injury; by ending up paralyzed, I let down the entire world of girl football players who dreamed of becoming me, someday. The jerks who said women should never play in the NFL were all vindicated by my accident. I failed all the husky football jock girls playing in Pop Warner, and if you give me this job, I will fail you, too.

I'm not coming to the Wisdom Palace, anymore. I don't belong. Todd is worthy. He belongs. He is big enough for this job. The others you've picked are so brave! They are the heroes. I am too jealous and little and angry and scared and sad.

I will always be grateful to you for giving me such an honor. I will never betray any of the secrets I learned in the Wisdom Palace. I will pray for all of you—true warriors—with everything I have. You are a great, brave lady, Ulena.

Sincerely,

Pepper

I hated writing such a wimpy letter. I hated myself. "Not only am I a total loser, I'm also a quitter!" I scolded myself. I lifted myself onto my bed, and cried and cried. I cried for myself, for the first time in a long time. I cried for the loss of my limbs, and the loss of my physical power. I cried for the loss of my feelings of invincibility, and the feeling I could do anything I wanted, if I put my mind to it. That was all crap. I didn't have that kind of power, anymore. I was one washed-up jock.

I didn't usually feel sorry for myself, except that night, I did. I spent all night crying and feeling sorry for myself, until the tears finally overtook me.

Mom says I was snoring when she came home. She woke me, briefly, and I saw the sorrow and love in her eyes. Knowing my mother the way I do, I know she knew I had suffered. She knows me so well! She said we would talk about it later, when she knew I was ready. To have a mother like her was the best gift of all, but somehow, I mumbled to her as I returned to sleep, I felt I'd let her down, too. She was like the Ultimate Mother of the Earth Core Tunnel people: this giant, brave mother who discovered the Sun Quartz Fields. What was I doing in this crowd of giants and heroes?

From the Earth Memories Archives
Compiled by Marla, Sea Faerie Keeper
Of Memories

"Oh, Pepper," Ulena said, sighing, reading Pepper's e-mail. Ulena closed her beautiful, sightless eyes, and felt what it feels like to doubt oneself at the very core. She knew the feeling well: to know you cannot do what God, or Country, or Goodness, have asked you to do, and to know you are just a little person the Creator falsely imagined was bigger.

Tears spilled the long distance from Ulena's chin to her clavicle. She remembered her own time of self-doubt. It was too painful! Ulena jolted Queen Rona from her sleep by telepathically shouting, "Rona! It is time for Pepper to visit Koba, and it is time for her to feel your belief in her, in the deepest chamber of her heart." Ulena then answered Pepper's e-mail.

Dear Pepper,

I once wrote the very same words you wrote. I wrote them to Rona, long ago. It is time, dear Pepper, for you to meet Rona, for it is Rona who soothed me when I wrote those words, long ago. Feel the love, not the pressure, of the thousands who love you. That love is what makes you stronger than anyone.

Love, Ulena

From the Earth Memories Archives
Compiled by Pepper McCullah,
Clan of the Fan-Feathered Brow
Earth Year 2030

I know I was asleep, because I woke up suddenly. My computer was on. I had turned it off before I went to bed, so my folks wouldn't read my sad letter. A short letter from Ulena warmed by chilly heart with the gentle empathy of her words.

I didn't have much time to think or feel anything, however, because my head started filling up with someone else's words booming, echoing, as in a giant lecture hall.

Queen Rona of Koba's voice bounced all over my aching head. "Pepper! We are finally going to meet. I want you to relax."

"Right." Snotty, yes, but I did not feel relaxed. I could feel Queen Rona smiling, inside my head. Then her telepathy-voice totally changed, and her voice became very melodic and soothing.

"Take a deep breath, Pepper, and imagine yourself swimming effortlessly in a liquid realm of peace. You are coming to visit us in Koba, deep in the River of Life, where only Ascended Masters of the Ages can dwell. Koba is a place of peace, of beauty, and of wonder, far below your oceans. You will be happy here, and you will be loved."

My head grew dizzy, and I felt it go thud! on my chest. My eyes were pointing toward the ground, and my closed eyeballs swirling around, down, down. I felt weightless and whole, and traveling freely.

I was flying again, and it felt great! The atmosphere around me felt heavier than before, almost liquid. White birds, the holy ibis birds in Nanu's story, traveled with me, upward, soaring, working their muscles hard to rise. They dove with me as well, deeply into the clear, turquoise waters of the ocean.

Just after penetrating the clear, warm waters, the ibis birds transformed into wildly colorful jellyfish. They were bright neon orange and pink, all around me. They never stung me, and I felt safe near them. Their movements were rhythmic, poetic, like beautiful dancers in designer dresses. They glowed a welcome to me, and hovered around, shining a pinkish-orange light and protecting me.

I looked down at myself, to see what sort of body I'd morphed into. There wasn't much of a body. I was very much like the jellyfish, except I was a glowing, turquoise blue. My form had taken the shape of the jellyfish, which is not very much of a form. I was transparent, and shimmering with rainbow-colored lights. My jellyfish form was like a shimmering designer gown, gauzy and free flowing.

Wandering deeper, I met a funny creature: half toad, half crabby old man. He had a big belly, and I instantly knew his name was Grimace Toad. (No, he was not wearing a nametag.) He smirked at me, and didn't say a word. His job, I deduced, was to guard the doorway leading to the River of Life. I felt glad they had a sense of humor here.

The jellyfish and I laughed together at the joke, and our laughter colored the ocean around us with neon colors. We floated onward, swimming effortlessly and gracefully. We came to a shining dome of pure crystal, surrounded by doors and walls of pure gold.

Poofo! I swam effortlessly through the crystal dome. Many see-through jellyfish forms greeted me. They floated with me (it didn't feel much like swimming—it was very graceful, floaty, and free) past incredible coral gardens. Huge, tangerine and neon-pink sea roses and sea sunflowers swayed a wavy greeting to us. The vibrant, orange and pink coral mingled with sun-yellow sea flowers in this magical, new world.

Beyond the breathtaking gardens, we entered a roofless, great hall, covered with tall, crystal spires. My gentle guides led me before another jellyfish form on a throne. Queen Rona. I knew it in an instant.

She was beautiful! Her long, black hair floated all around her like an inky cloud, and her aura glowed with radiant oranges and yellows and pinks. She had the hugest black eyes, almost like a fly's, or an alien's, and the rest of her was like a lacy, floaty jellyfish.

She radiated total love. The love emanating from her constant-sunset aura made my face hot. She spoke to me always from her eyes, telepathically.

"Pepper," she said to me in my head, in the softest, most loving voice I have ever heard. "Have you heard of the Living Goddess, Kuan Yin?"

"Yes, Queen Rona. The Living Goddess of Compassion, of course."

"I am Her royal sister, in this form, in this age, living in the River of Life with Ascended Masters beneath the bottom of the sea. Inspired by my sister, Kuan Yin, I have sworn to remain among Earth mortals until all suffering, for all humans, has ended. I know how you suffer when you doubt yourself. I know, dear Pepper. We have all suffered, doubting our own power, exactly as you have just now suffered. The greatest warriors always suffer the most doubt before their greatest battles. We sometimes refer to it as our own, personal Garden of Gethseminee. Remember the story of Jesus telling God, His Father, to give His destiny to someone else, because He did not feel up to the task of dying on a Cross?"

"Yes."

"And so it is with you. This battle is your destiny. It is the destiny of the Clan of the Fan-Feathered Brow, and has been for six thousand years. You are strong enough, and wise enough for this job, dear Pepper. You are filled with the love of hundreds of thousands of ordinary people who look up to you.

"Those little girls you feel you let down? They do not see it that way. They love you, and even now, they are training hard, to someday beat your records. See if you see anything except love for you, and determination on their faces."

She waved her lacy, jellyfish "arm", and a high school football game in progress appeared. Three girls on the team looked pretty darned good! The girl who won my heart instantly was the quarterback. Her sandy hair was in a ponytail that hung below her helmet, and behind her face mask were freckles. She was maybe in tenth grade. She tried to get a pass off to her receiver, but he was being blocked efficiently by the other side's corner back. She decided to run it. I couldn't believe it! She got about ten yards before some hulky dude tagged her. It warmed my heart, and brought back some really good times. I smiled, and the football game vanished.

"Pepper, that little quarterback has pictures of you all over her room. She will surpass you someday, I promise. She will surpass you through determination, of course, but, more than anything, she will surpass you because her love for you fills her with courage."

I saw all the TV cameras on the sidelines and I knew in my bones—well, in my jellyfish things—that what Rona said was true.

"Thank you, Queen Rona." I was giddy, and happier than I'd been in months. What a gift this queen had given me! There was a feisty high school quarterback girl out there who was going to go all the way! And she was doing it partly for me. Because of me, maybe! My life suddenly seemed important. I was important, maybe not a loser at all!

"Pepper, you're going to go further into your past. We're going to take you to meet your ancestors from the Red Land, Atlantis."

"Further back than Nanu? I thought she started the Clan of the Fan-Feathered Brow."

"She did, and you are her descendant, in a long line of noble warriors and mystics and scholars who lived all over Earth, at all different time periods that have led us here, to this Reunion of Noble Spirits from all the ages. But Nanu is the reincarnation of Re-ve, who was born to a priestess in Atlantis. She is fun, and you will love meeting her, and hearing her story."

"I do love hearing these stories, but hearing Nanu's story is what depressed me. I could never be as brave as she was."

Queen Rona's inky cloud of swirling black hair caught the orange and neon lights of her laughter. Her black alien eyes dove into mine. "You have her blood, Pepper. You are every bit as brave as she was, and when you meet your destiny, you will not flinch for an instant. History has chosen you wisely."

"So tell me about this 'Ray-vay'. It sounds French."

"So much of your language has survived from Mu and Atlantis. Yes, in its current French, 'Rever' means 'to dream.' Re-ve was her parents' dream for the future of Earth. But let her tell her tale, for she is a lively, wonderful spirit who reminds me very much of you."

Rona waved her magical, jellyfish arm, and the noisy sound of a horse's hooves galloping filled the air. I heard laughter that tinkled and splashed in orange and pink ripples all around us in the liquid air above our heads.

A magnificent white horse with a long, fuchsia and purple mane and tail, galloped into sight, above our heads. The laughing girl guided her huge, muscled horse into three full somersaults before adroitly guiding him downward, to our sides. Her horse was laughing, too.

She was a beautiful athlete! Maybe twelve years old and lean, she was very muscular. Wearing an ancient-looking robe, like the clothes you see on Greek or Roman statues, hers was very short, so it didn't interfere with her riding. Her thighs and legs were bare, as were her feet. Her legs and arms were strong. Her face radiated joy. She wore a golden band at her forehead; it looked like a lightweight crown, and served to bind her long, wild hair, which now shone purple from all her colored laughter in the liquid air.

"Rona, my Queen of Queens!" She yelled loudly, as if at a party. "You beckon me for the coming Reunion, yes? Or would you have Shima and me return to earthly bodies to do our part in the battle beforehand? We'd love that, and you know it!" She talked like a Viking, ready for battle.

"Re-ve and Shima, we will all be taking part in both the battle and the Reunion, but you will not be in the physical Earth space, Laughing Lady. Your job will be a spiritual one," Rona said, speaking softly and lovingly, as if to a child. The "laughing lady" frowned like the young girl she was.

Rona then waved toward me, to introduce me. "This is Pepper, from the Clan of the Fan-Feathered Brow. She is to play a pivotal part in the battle against the Greed Kings, but she needs you to help her remember her most distant past, just as you once guided her ancestor, Nanu, when you incarnated into her Egyptian form."

Re-ve frowned harder and said, "She's old, and she sits in a chair with wheels, all day."

I don't know if my jellyfish face blushed, but I felt that hot, prickly rash feeling sweep over my face. This spirit-kid was pissing me off. "I'm twenty-two!! That is not old! And everybody says it doesn't matter if I'm in a wheelchair! I mean, you don't see me in a wheelchair now, do you?"

I was fighting with an apparition! Fighting over my supposed destiny, which I'd been whining I was in no way prepared to face! And so I learned, in that instant, I did want to face this earth-saving destiny!

Re-ve laughed loudly, and again, the air all around her splashed with purple and neon pink colors and tinkling sounds. It was as if she read my mind, and what I'd just said was what she'd hoped I would say when she said those mean things. I probably will never get used to everyone in this realm being able to do things like that.

"Pepper! We are linked, you and I. We are both athletes. My mother was Makara, the greatest Healing Priestess in any Earth-age, and my father was Murakanda, a great, wise warrior whose lineage from the land of Mu was unbroken. In the ways of those times, my parents knew who I was as I grew inside my mama. Mama could rest her hand on her tummy and simply know me: she knew my spirit, who I had been, and who I would be. They knew I would someday spread the Light of Knowledge from our Red Land, in far away places they would never see. They taught me while I was still inside the womb. I was quiet, and paying attention to every teaching. And so they named me Re-ve, their Dream."

"She is not exaggerating about her parents' vast powers, Pepper," Rona said softly. 'Makara' in the ancient language holds 'Ma,' the word for feminine, and ka, which refers to the purple fire of total cleansing. Watch her as she was in her glory days, in Atlantis."

Rona waved her lacy arm, and a holograph arose, as if we were there, in Atlantis. We were in a room inside a cave made of rosy, red rocks, and glowing crystals covered the red rock walls of the cave. The room glowed brightly with pink, white, and golden crystals. A pool of hot, glowing, greenish-turquoise water that steamed slightly. Wonderful, musical sounds of lullaby-singing and laughter came from the pool's glowing waters. The water sang with joy; it was alive!

In walked a beautiful, extremely tall woman with long, thick, red, curly hair. "Mama!" Re-ve called out lovingly, like a young child as she looked at the vision.

Rona spoke. "This, Pepper, is Makara, the greatest Healer ever known on Earth. You are connected to her, down through the ages, through Re-ve, and through Nanu."

Makara wore a royal blue robe, and turned to wait for a moment while a very sick man was carried in on a stretcher. He was so weak, he could not lift his head.

Makara beckoned the sad relatives who carried him to lay him down on a glowing bed of clear, crystal quartz. She nodded at them, and indicated they should leave her alone with the sick man.

She sat, cross-legged on another glowing crystal bed across from him, and closed her eyes. After a few moments of deep meditation, a bright, white light burst from her heart, and filled her chest. The bright, white light rose to her neck, then filled her face.

Suddenly, a huge, bright light exploded from her head like lightning. It lit the man's whole body! It was incredibly bright; I had to shield my eyes. The flash lingered, and hovered over him for a moment. He rose, smiling, and bowed to her in thanks. She smiled at him radiantly, with pure love, and pure joy.

"Wow!" I said. Unbelievable, the power of this woman's loving energy. My own mother could do things like that. And Rona had said I was connected to her!

Re-ve wanted me to know more about her wonderful life in Atlantis. "Pepper, pay attention! I want to show you all the fun I had."

She was such a brat!

"Shima is my horse, and my beloved friend."

At the sound of his name, Shima tossed his colorful mane and nipped at Re-ve's dark hair with his big teeth.

Re-ve lifted her arm absent-mindedly to pat Shima's nose. She continued with her history. "The language still lives today as it did in Atlantis. Your Hopi Indians in the Southwest of America still use the word 'Shima' properly. It means 'Love'. My parents gave Shima to me as a gift of Love. Watch us race across the Red Land."

The lush green that grew in the valleys of Atlantis was a wonderful contrast to the bright red earth beneath the green. Beautiful canals made of white marble connected plots of land to each other, and giant, marble vases filled with hanging purple flowers draped into the fresh water of the canals.

Shima and Re-ve galloped to the edge of one canal and leaped high to cross it. Re-ve was laughing, and whooping loudly. Shima laughed a horse laugh, with his head back, and a big horsey grin. Re-ve held a red scarf high above her head as she and Shima galloped, up to a group of other children on their horses. All the children held different-colored scarves, and the laughing group suddenly began thundering down a red dirt road toward a finish line.

A handsome young man, younger than Re-ve, galloped up to her and smiled.

"Mudeen, my brother!" Re-ve shouted, clapping her hands.

Re-ve was focused on the finish line before her; her strong legs and arm muscles flexed as she pushed Shima harder. She held onto a silken, purple rope around Shima's neck. There was no harness or halter, or saddle. It was a magnificent display of athlete and horse, united in desire and spirit.

Re-ve and Shima were dead even with a boy on his beautiful, chestnut horse. He held a red, silken rope around his horse's neck with one hand, while twirling the rainbow scarf above him with the other. Re-ve and the boy smiled at each other for just a moment, before Re-ve surged ahead, to cross the golden finish rope first.

Re-ve laughed, and I laughed, too.

"Hurray for Re-ve!" I yelled. "Great show!"

Re-ve patted Shima, who nuzzled her hand. The movements spoke loudly to me in my heart, of the friendship between the girl and her horse. Re-ve smiled, then returned abruptly to my instruction.

"My father was Murakanda."

A gorgeous, dark-haired man, also extremely tall, came into our vision. Re-ve smiled at him widely, as he smiled at his adored little girl.

"His ancestors were from 'Mu,' and the line from Mu was unbroken. Everyone with ancestors from Mu had Mu in their name, and they were immediately blessed, and royal. 'Ra' is the masculine, and 'Ka' is the fire energy. My father was a great, wise warrior, who fought to keep the most ancient ways sacred. He and my mother were the most famous lovers of our time, because they'd loved each other through many lifetimes. Because they always knew each other in their new life, they never had to get reacquainted. They just picked up where they'd left off in the last life, and so their love grew, and all of Atlantis flourished, because of it.

"One Greed King created the legend in Atlantis saying that whenever they kissed, the fire in Earth's belly grew hotter, but, of course, their kisses had nothing to do with what would happen to Atlantis.

"They were such highly evolved beings, in touch with every crystal and stone in Atlantis, along with their powers. They understood the consciousness in all things, and the rocks and crystals spoke with them. My father taught me that minerals separate the seen realms from the unseen ones, so you can tap into their power to reach the unseen realms."

Rona interrupted, to make the import of this lesson clear to me. "Crystals, filled as they are with minerals, are crystallized forms of Pure Light Beings. That, Pepper, is the ancient secret Atlanteans understood. It is the source of vast power in this universe."

"I would've said that, Queen Rona," Re-ve said with a pout. "Anyway, as the Greed Kings' power, and Materialism, grew stronger on Atlantis, the crystals' power retreated. Atlanteans forgot their history, and the ley line cracks in Earth became clogged. Our collective unity of mind-spirit-heart became divided. Division was introduced by those who feed and prosper on chaos. Our giant island continent had been a fragile ecosystem, held together with united love and spirits, so the battle between body-mind materialism and heart-spirit intuition caused Earth to split, as well. Atlantis started to collapse and explode. Pieces of her broke off for months before the whole island went under.

"The last time I saw Mama and Da and Mudeen, they led me to the edge of the island that was very close to a chain of islands that had already broken off from the big island continent. Volcanoes were exploding all around us, and they held me one last time before putting me on Shima.

"They told Shima to leap high and far, from island to island, until we were safe. I did not want to leave them, and I cried a thousand tears. Da had never ignored my tears before, and I was angry, but he slapped Shima hard on his backside. Shima knew what he must do. He knew our destiny.

"As we flew into the air, I looked back to see my father put Mudeen in a boat heading east. Mama was crying into Mudeen's hair. Mudeen's boat sailed away, and I watched Da kiss my mother goodbye. I will never see another kiss like that again, not in a million lifetimes. She carried another child in her body, and together, Mama and Da put their hands on Mama's belly, which began to glow with a bright light. He then put Mama in a boat, with a few glowing crystals, and many scrolls of ancient knowledge, and sent her in a different direction—sailing toward what became the Faerie Isles in the Atlantic. Da stayed on, loading scrolls and stones and tablets filled with ancient knowledge, in the boats of priests and healers. He sent them in every direction, before he went down with the last of our great island.

"In Shima's saddlebag, Mama and Da had loaded scrolls of knowledge I was to carry into the new land. Shima and I ended up in Egypt, where I met with other survivors from Atlantis. Many of them also carried the lineage of 'Mu' in their names, as my father had. They hugged me hard, and called me their child. They were so glad to know the ancient knowledge would be remembered in this new land! I had carried the ancient knowledge of Light from the sun quartz crystals, and I retained some of my mother's healing ways. I carried the Atlantean knowledge of mind over matter, which we used to build our early temples to the sky, in Egypt."

"How old were you when you died?" I wondered, for she talked as if she'd never been anything but a child.

"Twelve. Pretty much as you see me now. I arrived in Egypt, and met with the others, my new 'Family of Knowledge,' as we called ourselves. We were filled with our purpose: we had beautiful wisdom from the Red Land to disseminate around this beautiful, new land. I shared my parents' light wisdom, and their healing wisdom. My new family celebrated many feasts to celebrate the keeping of our wisdom. We charged into the building of the new temples, using our minds and hearts and spirits.

"Just after we finished the Great Sphinx, the last of Atlantis sank, and huge floods covered the entire Earth. That's in your Bible. Then

I died. I was stung by a scorpion, of all things! Terrible, nasty creatures they are! Nothing is a coincidence, you know. When I reincarnated as Nanu, it was no coincidence that I learned the Isis ritual of
healing with scorpions, and my husband was a scorpion charmer! All
life is a magical gift, don't you think?" Re-ve asked.

"My life has become crazy-magical, almost too crazy magical to
believe, since I came to the Wisdom Palace that first time."

"So, Pepper, I am here to tell you that if a twelve-year-old girl can
change the history of the world above and below, certainly an old
lady like yourself can do the same. You see me now as Re-ve, and you
have Re-ve's DNA memory. You also have some of my mother's DNA
memory, and that of my father. I later returned as Nanu, your Clan's
first mother, and you have the brave Nanu's blood in you. In your
DNA is the memory of all that has passed, down through the ages.
My father was the greatest hero of all, and my mother was the most
loving healer. You have everything inside you, Pepper. Pieces of all of
us."

I laughed, and watched the liquid air all around me turn orange
and pink. "Okay, okay! Give me a spaceship, and some warrior
armor, and we'll go beat those Greed Kings! They've messed with
Earth for 10,000 years, and that is long enough!"

TRAINING BEGINS
IN THE WISDOM PALACE

From the Earth Memories Archives
Compiled by Pepper McCullah
Clan of the Fan-Feathered Brow
Earth Year 2030

Rona's royal husband, King Kanta, wore a gold crown nestled in his soft cloud of white hair. He carried a gold trident, symbol of the force of fire beneath the sea. Rona looked radiant as ever, in a royal blue gown, her black hair swirling all around her. Marla glowed, surrounded by an orange and pink, firey light.

Ulena was dressed in silver, which made her blind eyes silvery blue-green, high above her long, regal neck. Awesome! She told us to close our eyes, for she was about to charge the room with an electrical current, similar to the one my Atlantean ancestor Makara once used for healing.

Even behind my closed eyes, I felt the blast of blinding white light flash through the entire hall. Todd squeezed my hand, and I smiled. I could feel his excitement at finally taking part in the most technologically advanced war of all times: the war uniting spirits, minds, and hearts against dark, limited machines.

By now, we were getting used to strange, exciting things happening constantly, but nothing prepared us for the weirdness that happened next. With absolute suddenness, in the giant hall there suddenly stood six golden, twelve-foot tall, amphibian-looking creatures. They had fins, but stood upright.

Whoa! I nearly had a heart attack! I backed up my wheelchair, and was astounded that Todd moved forward, as if to protect me. Cheez, what a chumpy thing to do, I thought. These creatures could pick him and his wheelchair up, and eat him as a tiny snack.

Once the initial shock of their imposing size and strangeness evaporated, a wave of calm happiness went through me. Their black eyes, high above us, were huge, and kind. I felt myself wanting to dive into those giant, black orbs, for in each of the giant amphibian's eyes, there seemed to live an entire galaxy. Their clothing glowed, golden, as if it were made of light that had been woven with twenty-four-karat gold. They were glowing, golden beings. Once the initial shock of their imposing size evaporated, I felt happy, just being in their presence.

Ulena spoke telepathically to us. "It is an honor to introduce these Zoloatons. They are the only beings in all the galaxies who have never once been conquered, despite the many, many Reptilians who have tried. They are so highly evolved, that when they are attacked, they unite as a race and vibrate with compassion, until all their beings, and their entire planet, become invisible. Their beautiful lives on Zoloat, in the distant future, are harmonious and peaceful. Zoloat is blue and green and warm, like Earth. Zoloatons' wish is for Earth humans to live as they do, a life without hate, without fear, and without hunger. They have answered the Goddess Kuan Yin—our Koban Queen Rona's sister—who asked them to come here from the distant future in order to teach humans to live without suffering, so she may finally go home to heaven. Earth people outside the Wisdom Palace, including the Greed Kings, have no idea of the Zoloatons' existence, so you will never speak of them."

Ulena's silvery eyes watered. She smiled, and spoke now with her mouth. "We are so blessed to have them among us for a short while. Not many beings in all the galaxies have ever seen them, not in

400,000 years! Their lessons will give you the greatest weapons, Vibrational Compassion and Wisdom, as well as their secret, ancient arts of War for the Peaceful Warriors. They will speak to you in your minds and your hearts, so open your hearts fully in order to hear them.

"The King and Queen, as well as Marla, the most illustrious Keeper of Memories, and myself, are here to learn right beside you. We are all humble students of these, the greatest and most successful Warriors of all the galaxies, and all the ages!"

One of the scary-huge amphibians stepped forward, and gentle, funny words formed in my head. The words tickled! A Zoloaton was speaking telepathically in my head.

"What a build-up, Ulena! We're just your everyday, normal Zoloatons, doin' our jobs! Seriously, though, we love this planet, and we love the humans, and we feel you Wisdom Retrievers are ready for our lessons."

I smiled at Todd, whose blue eyes were bulging.

It was hard to say if this was a he or a she, as the voice wasn't male or female. The "voice" vibrations inside my head felt gentle, ancient, and soothing.

The Zoloaton continued. "I have come here from your distant future, to help Earth reach her final destiny of joy. Your land and people have suffered so long, and I am here to guide you to her final phase of Harmony. My name is Rakama, Heartkeeper of the Spirit of Cleansing Fire."

He parted his glowing, golden robe, and we gasped. The Zoloaton showed us a dancing, boiling flame of purple fire, magically gyrating inside a vaguely human-shaped heart.

"Since you're all paying such close attention, there's this fun little trick I do," the Zoloatohn said inside my head.

We started laughing when the purple flame inside the heart changed its shape into that of an Arab girl, whose dance went from classic mideastern to a wiggy hip-hop.

"There have always been, on your planet, Mystery Schools teaching you the Ways of Within. Our knowledge is that which you have always had, inside yourselves, and within the wisdom teachings of all the ages. For many different reasons, Earth people have come within an arm's reach of all that we Zoloatons know, many times, but it was never yet your time to know fully.

"Still, many of you have had this wisdom inside you, all along, and all down through the Ages of Stupidity. I want to tell you about the Inuit people, natives of the icy lands to the north. Just last century, an Inuit man would go out to hunt the whale for food, and his wife would lie on the ice of the shore as her man paddled away to hunt. She would go into a meditative trance, and bring the whale to her man, who was by now far at sea. She used the developed powers of her mind, heart, and spirit in the ancient ways of wisdom, to coax the whale toward her man. These people were thought to be primitive, but they were using the ancient wisdom their more mechanically advanced relations had forgotten.

"Over and over, in Earth's story, there have been natural cataclysms. These are wars between Materialism and the Spirit. Wisdom Evolution would be obliterated in the cataclysms, and Earth people would have to begin again, an existence of mere survival, before again re-learning the Ways of Wisdom Within. What is different now is that, in the great cataclysm brought from heaven by Gonaquadet, those humans who went inside the very womb of Earth to live next to her heart retrieved more ancient wisdom than ever before.

"You have evolved greatly. You have become an old race—survivors of many cataclysms—and it is time to form the missing Wisdom links, in your bodies' DNA, and in your minds, hearts, and spirits.

"Your people lost much, in the terrible cataclysm of 2012. Only your compassion and wisdom kept Earth alive, and the compassion and wisdom you gained from this trauma has readied you for what now lies ahead. You are the seeds, born from a cataclysm, who will remake Earth into a wondrous Field of Compassion, where all dreams are possible, for all your people."

Tears glittered in Ulena's silvery blind eyes. "I have waited all my many lives for this moment," she whispered. Her face beamed, and she breathed deeply. Smiling broadly to herself for a moment, she savored the realization of her longtime dream. Then, her smile faded, and she frowned.

There was trouble she must mention. "Rakama, are you aware that Marla met with Tronot, and he intends to decimate the entire Wisdom Palace with nuclear power?"

"We got that guy so covered," Rakama said. He laughed. "Right now, all Zoloatons are using massive, vibrational brain waves of compassion to put up a force field that no puny nuclear weapons could ever hope to penetrate."

Another jolly, giant amphibian creature stepped forward. Raising gigantic arms, it shouted, "It's showtime! Watch this, Earth People!" The entire, gigantic hall exploded in an electrical flash of white light. Again, like a flash of sizzling lightning from a summer mountain storm in the Rockies, the entire hall flashed and burned with white, electrical light.

"I am Butara, the Great Teacher, and that is your first lesson. Every single one of you can do this, no sweat. In every single cell of your body, there dwells 1.74 volts of electricity. You have about a quadrillion cells in your body, which means, if you put all your ability to focus on it, each one of you can direct a 1.74 quadrillion volt charge of electricity into wherever you want it to zap. Got it?"

We nodded, feebly. It was a big concept.

"No, I mean, are you beginning to understand the incredible power each and every one of you has to energize this planet? No feeble nods, please. I want to hear you shout, like the powerful, electrical forces of light that you are!"

"Yes!" we shouted, somewhat feebly.

"I can't hear you," the amphibian sing-sang in our heads.

"YES!" We shouted, with all our strength, laughing.

We watched, spellbound, as Butara hummed like an old monk. His/her entire body started shaking, and the room was filled with this massive humming, like a giant swarm of killer bees. Butara's smooth, golden face was glowing with radiant joy, and he/she started floating, and lifting gently off the ground. While hovering above us, Butara simply, suddenly vanished before our eyes.

A big whooshing sounded behind us. "Does this look fun, or what?" Butara asked us in our heads, with a whooshing sound. Then we "heard" it to the right side, then to the left. "Hee-heee-hee-hee, Wheeeee!" The happy being shouted in our heads, as the whooshing sound did loop-de-loops all around us.

Todd was hyped, and bounced up and down in his chair, like a little kid. "We're gonna learn to do this?"

"Yeh, Mon, why not?" we heard in our heads, while the whooshing sound came from Todd's shoulders.

Todd giggled. "That tickles! Stop! Hee, hee, hee. I surrender! You win wars by tickling people? Hee, hee, hee, show me some mercy, Dinosaur Being!"

A huge belly laugh echoed all over the hall. "Laughter, Earth People, is the force of Freedom being sung. Never forget that. Your Earth dolphins laugh so loud at night, we in the distant cosmos can't get to sleep sometimes! Those dolphins have big freedom in their hearts. We love them so much, we keep some in every dimension."

The golden, giant amphibian bounded in front of us, visible again. "Wanna do it, Earth People?"

"Yes!" we yelled, laughing.

"You know, these tricks are not just for games and winning wars. Here's a little motivational secret: if you become masters at harnessing the 1.74 quadrillion volts of electrical energy each one of your bodies is capable of generating, you will be able to heal any illness, anywhere, on anybody. Who do you think that includes?"

"Ourselves?" I asked, wanting it to be so.

"Most absolutely, Pepper McCullah. You get good enough at this, and you can zap away that wheelchair in a heartbeat. The power is all stored up inside yourself, waiting to be released."

The room became really silent, but, antsy with a crazy excitement, we shifted around in our wheelchairs. The room filled with joyful, hopeful buzzing. Everybody started dreaming aloud, and raising their voices in anticipation. It was a moment I hope I remember always: hope is a rush!

Oddly, I froze in my excitement. I wanted this, more than anything I've ever wanted. Saving the world was glorious and noble, and I wanted to be a part of it, for sure. What I never seemed to be allowed to say to anyone, but what I wanted more than anything in this world, was to run again.

I'd spent so much time being told to "get used to" my new life in a wheelchair. My counselors, and Frank, my physical therapist, are the most wonderful people. I understand their mission is for us to get used to our disabilities and capabilities so we can move on and lead the most productive, happy, creative lives possible. But in the core of my heart, I never bought the "get used to it" line. I couldn't tell anyone, because I'd get the "face the facts" lecture, but I always believed there was some untapped power within myself that could accomplish absolutely anything.

I knew the legend of my mom in the Earth Core Tunnels, how she'd healed a kid who broke his spine. I knew she could have healed me, if she'd chosen to, and someday, I knew I'd finally spit it out and ask why she hadn't. Well, duh, my spine had to be open so I could meet my destiny at the Sun Quartz Fields. Still, wouldn't a mom who could heal her child just go and do it? I would.

I fully believed, somewhere inside me was the power to make myself whole, and completely healed. I'd seen the ancient Makara—my own ancestor—perform healing magic. Nanu could heal, and my mother, Alaiya, could heal as Makara once healed, using only the light force within her. Now, this golden, twelve-foot tall amphibian from Zoloat was telling me I also had the same light force within myself. It was I who'd been right, the whole time! My insides fluttered. I had to "return to Earth," and listen to the Zoloaton. He/she was going to begin instruction.

"It took me about a thousand years to learn all this stuff, but I'll see if I can speed up the process for you. It all begins with the breath. Breath is everything: the bridge between the conscious and the unconscious. You're going to learn a thousand, ancient ways to breathe that will change who and what you are in relation to the world around you. Your breath is the highway that will take you to your own, unlimited powers, and unite you with the Oneness of the Universe. You kids are gonna learn to breathe new life, and new reality, into your entire being, and the world around you. All your homework will be about breath, and you'll be doing a variety of breathing exercises. Got it?"

We did get it, and, over the next several weeks, along with everything else going on, we learned a thousand breathing techniques and exercises. These techniques had taken years of study for holy men and women down through the ages to learn, but we didn't have years.

Todd and I enjoyed all the breathing lessons; they took us to a deeply magical place inside ourselves. Still, we wanted to be involved in more of an active, physical sport—learning sword-throwing, maybe—so sometimes we were cranky and impatient. Of all the students, we were probably the most disruptive, rustling around in our chairs. He'd hold my hand and make funny faces at me, and I'd giggle like a child.

We learned to fill our body with huge, burning light, using only our breath. With that incredible skill, we could shoot the light from our Third Eye, illuminating our way in space: very handy, like a flashlight, only both your hands are freed! We also learned to take in with our breath the magic of reading the thoughts of others. We worked hard, for ten hours a day, for ten weeks, mastering breath techniques.

One day, after performing our acquired breath and meditation techniques, we were summoned by Butara for a special lesson. "Okay, Everybody, you've worked hard. I feel your power, and it's bound with the power of all the ancient and ascended masters. It's time to party hard. First, I want you to get really, really comfortable, and breathe in your Earthly oxygen deeply. It's gorgeous stuff, this Earth oxygen. Famous, you know, all over the galaxies. Breathe out, and let go of all tensions. Breathe in, and let your focus rest upon your heart. Breathe out, and imagine there is a beautiful temple right there, in your heart. Feel your heart grow, to accommodate this temple. The temple is made entirely of luminous, pink quartz, and could seat as many people as you feel around you now. Your heart is vast, and limitless."

The Zoloaton continued, much as Ulena always did, when she guided our meditations, except this one went deeper. I don't remember exactly what the Zoloatohn said or did to get us there, but I felt lighter and freer than I have ever felt. I felt myself float upward, and fly. I wasn't a morphed bird, like before; it wasn't that kind of flying. I became lightness itself, as if I were suddenly a flower petal, floating on a light breeze. Utter weightlessness was the most liberating feeling I'd ever known.

Butara said, "As you float upward, continue living in your heart. Explore the vastness, and the power, of all the love your heart generates. Now, you are all about twelve feet off the ground, so I'm going to help you lower yourselves, and gently return to the ground."

What a shock! We couldn't help it; we all opened our eyes. Our bodies really were twelve feet above the ground! Eighteen empty wheelchairs sat below. We had done the lift-off without them! When we realized we were floating around in the air on our own power, we lost confidence, and started falling.

The amazing Butara flew around the room, catching all eighteen of us in his/her huge, golden arms before we could fall. It is hard to describe the peace of resting in this giant palm. What a great first lesson! I wanted more.

Butara read my mind. I was finally starting to getting used to everyone doing that.

"Pepper, you will know it all, before you go to the Sun Quartz Fields. I promise. First, all you wheelchair warriors need to meet your crews. Get acquainted, and I'll be back for more flying and disappearing lessons, and more cool stuff culled from thousands of years' worth of wisdom. Ta-ta for now!"

Butara, and his/her giant friends vanished in an instant, laughing as they whooshed around and above us invisibly. How could I have even thought of bailing on this amazing, magical blast of an adventure!

WISDOM LESSONS OF THE AGES

From the Earth Memories Archives
Compiled by Marla, Sea Faerie Keeper
Of Memories

Watching Pepper and the others learn the first lessons of mind over matter brought back ancient memories. I wore the body of a beautiful young woman—much like Pepper, or Nanu, long ago—in the Land of the Immortal Serpent, my heart's home of Mu, when I first saw the lessons being learned. After Mu broke apart and sank, I watched from my form as a Sea Faerie, while transplanted Wisdom Elders from Mu taught the ancient lessons of the heart and its electrical magnetic powers to Atlanteans. As a Sea Faerie Keeper of Wisdom, I gloried in the Wisdom Elders of Mu who journeyed from Mu to a beautiful land in the mountains of Asia—Tibet—to keep the wisdom alive there. I went above, in the form of a temple servant, to live on the holy Ganges River, in India, while holy men studied and taught each other the same lessons of Wisdom.

It is always the same lesson—taught, forgotten, and re-taught: the Lessons of the Heart's Almighty Power, and the limitless power of the soul when body and mind, heart and soul are united in love and light. On the winter solstice of Earth's year 2030, the forces of light from all over the universe—above and below—will be so powerful, the Wisdom Lessons will be etched forever on the hearts of humans, like tattoos or cattle brands (dreadful, ancient human practices that can be found in my "Dreadful Human Practices, Down Through the Ages" text). Etched deeply into the human heart by the ignited power of the Sun Quartz Fields' return to dazzling life, the Wisdom Lessons will remain in the human heart, finally and forever. Humans will no longer create chaos and suffering to entertain themselves. They will be free.

WE MEET OUR CREW

From the Earth Memories Archives
Compiled by Pepper McCullah
Clan of the Fan-Feathered Brow
Earth Year 2030

Todd and I met Arinne first. She was a wonderful contrast to me, physically. My skin is olive-toned, and I'm muscular and large boned, as any football player should be. Arinne was a tiny Olympic gymnast in her teens, and her wheelchair seemed to swallow her body. Her skin was very fair, and her hair strawberry blonde. I loved her eyes, which were Irish Sea blue, but more than the color, I loved the way those eyes always seemed to know the next wonder that lay in store for us. She had that awesome, psychic gift of knowing past and future; I felt it when she looked at me. It was as if she knew my whole past by reading it in my eyes. She knew where I was right now in life, and she knew where I was going: all with one, thick look into my eyes.

Her voice, with her beautiful Irish accent, danced and tinkled as she introduced herself. "You and I are connected, Pepper, as Makara of Atlantis began my Clan: the Clan Beyond the Mists."

I gasped. Although thousands of years had passed, I could see Makara in Arinne's face. The big, curly hair had lightened in color since Atlantis, but its unruly force remained. The light behind the blue eyes remained, and the long, feminine nose. The gentle power in Arinne's face was so like Makara's! I stared at her, as if looking at a lost, distant ancestor. Incredible! Arinne's way was wise, like Makara's.

Arinne smiled at how taken I was with the recognition. She seemed to already have the inner sight that Ulena and Rona and all our coaches had, and began to respond to my thoughts. "While volcanoes and earthquakes ripped Atlantis apart for the final time, Makara fled in a boat with her healing crystals and holy wisdom tablets from Mu that Murakanda had given her. Sailing west, Makara landed in Britain, on the holy isle, carrying Murakanda's baby within her. Priestesses on the Faerie Isle knew of her coming, and she was welcomed with open arms. She who came from the Red Land, and who carried a child of Mu, was invited into the temples to teach all she knew. Makara embraced the ancient Goddess in Britain, and lived happily with the holy priestesses and faeries, there. She practiced the Goddess rites, and lived beyond the mists. She and her daughter, Ariel, began a new, matriarchal clan, the Clan Beyond the Mists. Her new clan—my clan—fled to Ireland to escape the savage Saxons, and we've been there ever since.

"My clan has been filled with healers and scholars for thousands of years." She looked down at her wheelchair, without any bitter irony over what she'd just said, and smiled. "This is only a temporary state, and I am grateful for it. I have learned a lot about my inner strengths, living in this chair. It is true, what they've told us—our broken spines allow better communication with the Earth through the ley lines, which are the cracks in the earth that lead to the earth's energetic core."

I had so much to learn, about so many things! My mother, Alaiya, knew all these ancient things, and she'd studied endlessly, all the time when we lived in the Earth Core Tunnels. I remembered some, but if I'd paid better attention when she'd tried to teach me, I'd know so much more. I began to appreciate the enormity of my mother's patience with me.

Arinne was beautiful to watch as she told about her people. "Our clan was prepared for the Great Cataclysm of 2012. We'd trained for it for hundreds of years. My parents knew of the secret caves below the floor of the Irish Sea, formed eons ago by huge, hollow tunnels of lava. We took many books, and animals, and plants, along with food we had dried and canned, down below the floor of the sea. We lived there four years. I was a newborn infant, and don't remember much of it except the smell of the sea from below. Smell is our most ancient sense. I don't remember the horrible, horrible shaking as the entire planet of Earth retched. When we emerged, there was nothing left. You are lucky, Pepper and Todd. America is large, so a chunk of it remains. Two hundred of us emerged onto a tiny heap of stones that had once been a gloriously beautiful country.

"When I found I had a talent for gymnastics, and was asked to join a tiny Olympic team, I was rebelling against my family's ancient line of scholars. I had to do it, though, to represent my lost country. It was beautiful, in 2024, the first Olympics competition since the cataclysm, to live in the Olympic Village with other survivors of countries that existed no more on land. These countries lived so brilliantly in the hearts of the athletes. I was proud to represent the lost, glorious land of Ireland, a land I never really saw. I was born far below the sea, in 2012. But the beauty of the Emerald Isle lives within me, in my DNA, and in my most ancient memories.

"I think a part of my father was glad when I fell from the rings and broke my spine. He is so proud of me now, in my role here as Wisdom Retriever." Arinne laughed, and I swear, her laugh reminded me of the laugh of Re-ve. "Glory Be, I've talked so much! That's one thing about the Irish that lives on forever: the Irish knack for dominating conversations with very long-winded stories!"

For the first time in my life, I felt I had a sister. I'd always felt like an oddball human, growing up with two wolf pup-brothers. My brothers were constantly mauling me and cuffing me and rolling and punching me. We had fun, but being part of a wolf pup litter was wild! Arinne and I connected immediately, in an ancient way; it was quietly, deeply fun. She was a real girl, wise and gentle, and we were bound by ancient DNA, and ancient memories I would someday learn to retrieve. I felt dazzled by her quiet wisdom, and a determination stirred in me, a determination to become as wise as Arinne. I made a mental note to apologize to my beautiful mother for not paying enough attention to all her lessons about our ancient clan, and the ancient wisdom. I would ask her to try again, the next time I saw her.

The next member of our crew was Tamdin, a mountain climber from Tibet. When he wheeled into our group and looked at me, my heart was lit with happiness, for in his face, I could already see the part of his story that was connected to me. (This was a good thing, because Tamdin was not so fond of talking as Arinne!)

Tamdin smiled at me, as if he knew me, down through the ages. He had black, shiny hair, and a huge, beautiful smile. His eyes were slanted, calm, and a luminous black. "Pepper McCullah. The leader of my ancient clan was Mudeen, son of Murakanda and Makara. Re-ve was Mudeen's sister, and she reincarnated into Nanu, mother of your clan."

"I can see in your face the resemblance between you and Mudeen and Murakanda," I said.

"You honor me. We know that Murakanda sent his wife to the west, his daughter, Re-ve, to the south, and his son Mudeen was put on a boat headed east. Our legend says he told Mudeen and his boat crew to find the Happy Mountains of Tibet, and to watch for him, for he would return to Earth a monk. Everyone would know him, he told his weeping son.

"Murakanda incarnated into Tonpa Dorje, Tibet's famous and holy monk. My clan, begun by his son, Mudeen, is the Clan of the Highest Peaks. Tonpa remembered his life as Murakanda, and spread the wisdom and teachings of Mu, all throughout the monasteries of Tibet. Murakanda is still a great legend in my country, as is Tonpa. In

Tibet today, we still believe there are many stone tablets of wisdom hidden in the bellies of the mountains. It is why I became a mountain climber, and why my misfortune of falling from the mountain resulted in my great fortune: being invited here."

Todd wheeled himself up to Tamdin, and shook his hand. "It is so great to meet you! I read all about you, when I used to dream of climbing in the Himalayas. I read about your amazing talent for finding ancient stone tablets of wisdom buried deep in high mountain caves. I dreamed of climbing with you, someday, but my coach never let me do it. He said it was too dangerous!" He laughed, looking down at his useless legs. "Now, I don't do much climbing. Tamdin, what was it like in Tibet, during the 2012 cataclysm?"

Tamdin had the whitest teeth I'd ever seen, and an inner light that made his face golden. "We were rejoicing, for one whole year, because the Dalai Lama had returned safely to Tibet in 2011. All Tibetans thought we would burst from so much happiness! For one year, our whole life was prayers and celebrations, in all the temples. There was no crime in Tibet, that year: only joy, and love, and compassion. I was only nine when the Dalai Lama returned, but I will never forget the Procession of Blossoms in Lhasa, and the joy on all the faces. His face was the most beautiful sight I'd ever seen: so gentle, and wise.

"But the holy men, praying with thanks to God all day and night, knew the Earth, and her changes. Lamas are scholars, and they had studied the prophecies. When you live so close to Earth as lamas and monks do, you communicate easily with her. When you sleep with your head on her breast each night, your heart beats with the heart of your mother, Earth. The monks told our people exactly what would happen, and our people listened. The Dalai Lama listened, and the people listened to him. All the people of Tibet streamed into the temples deep inside the holy, ancient caves, miles below the surface. We took yaks, who gave us everything, and we took rice, and chilies, and fires. The monks knew the secret, ancient pools of water that would give us life, and health."

He paused, and, although he prepared to tell us of a terrible catastrophe, his face retained its golden look of complete happiness. "We held hands, and prayed for compassion to help us go to the next life happy. We were not afraid to die, for we had love and compassion in our hearts. Our lives were in peak joy. That is a rough translation. I hope you understand."

We laughed. Todd said, "We understand, Tamdin. It sounds pretty good."

"We sang, we chanted, and we prayed. I remember mostly joy, in the ancient caves below. Many people died, of course, when the earth began to shake for days. Volcanoes, fires, crumbling mountains—well, you know. You had the same everywhere. Some cave temples remained, fully intact. I clung to my father and mother, who prayed with me the whole time. Snuggled into my parents, with my brothers and sisters, feeling my mother's warm breath, and hearing my father's strong voice, I was not afraid to die. I made a promise to God, Buddha, Tara—She is Goddess of Heaven—and Kuan Yin, Goddess of Compassion—that if I survived, I would climb the mountains that had been ripped open, to search for the 'terma,' which is the ancient treasure of wisdom I knew, even at that young age, was there. I kept my promise, and found many ancient stone tablets of wisdom, dating back 70,000 years. They were stone tablets from Mu, the Land of Immortal Serpents, telling a student how to use the Great Divine Force within oneself in order to control the forces of Earth. Then I met a crevasse. It snapped my spine, two years ago. Of course, there is no coincidence: I learned this, then my spine opened itself so I could serve Earth better."

We were very quiet until Arinne spoke. "I, like you, feel blessed with what has happened, Tamdin, and I now feel blessed to be in your crew," Arinne said, with deep feeling.

Whoa! Major electricity passed between them when they turned and looked fully into each other's faces. Like a dream: the two descendants of maybe the two greatest lovers of all time had clearly reincarnated into Tamdin and Arinne, and they'd just passed the biggest juice bar of electricity I'd ever experienced. It was hard to doubt, in that instant, that they were the reunited souls of Murakanda and Makara. Something huge sizzled between them! None of the rest of us breathed. Finally, I had some understanding of the power of love, and how it really might be possible to chemically change the course of Earth if this kind of electrical power could be unleashed and focused.

In this mission, the magic would never stop. Every time I thought, "this has to be the most magic I will ever experience in my life," something bigger happened. In that moment, while all this electrical current between Arinne and Tamdin was lighting up our chamber, I realized how much I loved my life. Arinne and Tamdin both talked about the "blessings" their accidents had bestowed upon them, and now, I agreed. I was the luckiest young woman alive, and I loved myself, and my life, with my whole heart.

The next person in our crew to introduce himself was Micah. A Hopi Indian he'd grown up in the mountains of Arizona, near Prescott. Micah had long black hair, and big, muscled arms. Micah is famous all over the world because of the huge, magnificent statues he has created from rock on his native land. I had admired his work for years, because the two best galleries in Tahoe each had one of his sculptures. I remembered reading of his accident; while climbing in the Sandia Mountains for stone to carve, he'd fallen, and broken his back. I remember the beautiful rock sculpture he carved afterward, telling the story of his fall. A beautiful eagle watched him fall, and the sculpture was named, "Falling into the Light of Darkness."

"It is an honor to meet you, Micah," I said. "I've admired your sculptures for a long time."

Micah blushed. "Thank you. I am the only sculptor in my family. My mother says if I'd stuck to making baskets and painting like the rest of my famous family, I would not have gotten hurt. But the rocks have always cried out to me, and every sculpture evolved because a rock would cry out to me, 'I have a story to tell. You must come and release the story within my heart.' I only do as the stone directs me." He blushed again.

"We are lucky to have a Hopi with us," Arinne said. Her blue eyes sparkled, and her wild curls danced. "You who know the stones so well, will steer us into the heart of the Sun Quartz Field. Wasn't it the Hopi whose leaders walked for hundreds of miles, a hundred years ago, in the 1940's, warning the United States Government of the ancient Hopi prophecies?"

"Yes." He nodded, and smiled. "I am half Hopi, and my Hopi grandfathers walked from Arizona to Washington, D.C., to try to make the U.S. Government people listen. The Hopi were scorned for years, and not allowed to speak to Congress, and then, when the Hopi messengers persisted, they were finally allowed to speak, but they spoke to no one. Congress was not in session. But their words were recorded, and I am proud to be Hopi, for my grandfathers spoke of the relentless plunder of Mother Earth for the sake of profit, and how our Mother, Earth, would need to purify herself of toxicity. The words were recorded, telling of a huge cataclysm that would occur in the first quarter of this new millennium, in 2012. It was our prophecy, handed down from thousands of years ago.

"Our people came from the islands of Mu, from water, many thousands of years ago. It is said the seven Kumara brothers led my people across seven of Mu's islands as they were exploding. As we settled in this beautiful new land, we kept our memories alive. We knew even then the Great Purification that would come. We were not surprised by the cataclysm, and we were not afraid. We'd known for so long it was coming. Many Hopi died in their community kivas, but they died with peace, and love for their Great Mother. They died happy for their Mother, who was finally cleansing herself, as our prophecy had foretold. Our people died knowing they would return, in their next lives, to the better, cleansed world of love and happiness. We call this new world, the Final World." He closed his big, deep eyes, and smiled at the vision behind those eyes. Tears fell from behind the lids.

"Because my father was a famous Navajo healer, and my mother was a Hopi teacher, we were invited by a group of scientists from Los Alamos to go two miles below the surface of the earth, to live, and pray, and help the Earth prepare for the Final World, beyond the purification time.

"My calling from Mother Earth has always been to listen to the stones, to hear their mineral hearts beat. To be an artist is only to be receptive to Beauty, and, as the Navajo say, to walk in Beauty always. It is an honor to be here, with you. We will use my gift of open heart listening to build the new world. It will be the best world yet."

Micah turned to me, and his gaze felt warm as the sun. "Pepper, my clan is the Clan of Rock and Sun, the same as your grandmother-by-marriage, Noni. Noni was her nickname, which meant 'Pink Flower that Heals all Life,'" he said, smiling. "Pink Flower was my grandmother."

My face opened with this giant grin. "Grandma Noni! Micah, this is so great!" I shouted, and squeezed his hand.

"Your grandmother Pink Flower had a son who helped with the birth of your mother, Alaiya, and our clans were united in spirit that day of her birth. Pink Flower's son was my Navajo father, Pollen Breath. He was named because of legends before his birth, saying he would bring peace to everything in his path, just from breathing. When my Hopi mother saw him, she told me she knew in one second he was her destiny."

Just as I was thinking what an incredibly uplifting guy Micah was, beautiful music began, and everyone fell silent. Our sixth and final crewmember was weaving a magically haunting tune on her fat wooden flute. By the time she finished, we were all in a floaty trance.

"My ancestors came from the Red Land—Atlantis—Micah, and we also prophesied, for thousands of years, the 2012 cataclysm," Danu, our final crewmember, said. "My people are the Mayans, and I was named after Danuih, Goddess of Earth in Atlantis."

Everyone shook hands all around. Danu was beautiful, with the hugest black eyes I'd ever seen above-ground. She was quiet in an unearthly way; I could picture her spending days alone in a rainforest.

"Wow, we're all so connected! 'Danu' was also the name of an ancient Norse goddess," Todd told Danu with great enthusiasm.

Danu smiled, and blushed. "Because my people knew the exact date the cataclysm would occur, we did not lose too many Mayans. Our numbers were so little, to begin with," she smiled sadly. "We had started building our cataclysm caves deep below the rainforests hundreds of years before, and all my people were saved. I was a baby in the caves, but the stories of life in the caves are sweet stories. As a baby, I learned the ancient history of my clan—The Forest Clan. The Ancient Father of our clan was Bromand, a great musician, whom you met, Pepper, inside the volcano. We are musicians, and we know the magic of opening hearts with music."

"Bromand was a babe," I said quietly, winking at Danu.

Danu laughed. "I have seen him, too, in the volcano. He was handsome," she giggled. Her face then clouded. "I was born lame, with my spine open in the middle. Everyone tells me that a great energy force and bright light always came from my spine, and seared holes in my baby clothing. Mama said it was because I was born in the year of the cataclysm. The wise grandfather of my clan prophesied to my mother that my open spine was a great gift, because my music, and my knowing, would someday bring attention to the Wisdom Retrievers. Grandfather told my mother I would play a great part in building the new world.

"Coming out from the caves, my people were saddened by the death and destruction, but when you know what will happen for thousands of years, you are prepared. We had taken many plants and animals below, into the caves. For decades before Gonaquadet, my people had nurtured a rainforest below the earth. They had prepared for the rebuilding after Gonaquadet, and they gave thanks for three days when we emerged, for allowing us to create the final world from the ashes of the old world. It was the music of my clan, on flutes and drums, that reawakened the life force of the forests from beneath the ashes."

"We are one great crew!" Todd shouted. "This is so incredible, because each of us has an amazing gift, and an amazing heritage. We rock!"

Todd was so Todd, I thought. He told us his history.

"Mine is the Clan of the Frozen Fields, and we can trace our ancestors all the way back to some traveling merchants from Mu who were trading with people in ancient Scandinavia when Mu went down. Lillith is the ancient Mother from Mu who began the Clan of the Frozen Fields."

I remember Lillith! I thought excitedly. She was the white haired lady with the serpent I'd first met when all this began, on my first astral vacation, in the volcano! She was with Bromand, Danu's ancestor.

"I come from a long line of Scandinavian physicists," Todd said, "and physicists understand the principles behind the vast wonder of life. I understand the ancient, sacred geometry, and the formulas written in ancient runes that will help us find the physical heart of the quartz fields." He stopped, and smiled. I thought to myself what a great team captain he was. He shared his thoughts with us, as we sat in a circle. All eyes were on his excited, blue eyes: my green eyes, Arinne's bright blue eyes, and Tamdin, Micah, and Danu's black eyes.

Todd continued. "They chose this crew well: Danu has the music to unblock our hearts, awaken the Light Beings, and transport us. I can shout the chants from the ancient runes to waken the Light Beings. Micah and Tamdin, you can speak with, and listen to, the souls of the Light Beings inside the crystals in the Sun Quartz Fields. Arinne has studied all the ancient legends. Deep within her is the knowing of the Light Beings. She is in charge of remembering, and she will show us all how to remember. She will sing the memories. Pepper is our warrior: she will be joined with the spirit of her clan mother, Nanu, in the final battle with Tronot. Working together, there is nothing this crew can't do!"

THE TESTS BEGIN

From the Earth Memories Archives
Compiled by Pepper McCullah
Clan of the Fan-Feathered Brow
Earth Year 2030

All the Wisdom Retrievers were assembled in the Great Hall. The sun was bright outside, and the pink quartz walls lit with brilliant sun dazzled the eyes with golden-rosy light. Ulena lifted her beautiful face to the warm glow. Her eyes were closed, but she seemed to "see" the beautiful, colored light with her whole being. All of us watched her, and a feeling of love for Ulena united us. It was easy to love Ulena!

She began, "The tests will simulate the Fear Battles. It is the Fear Battles, I think, that will win the war between The Wisdom Retrievers and the Greed Kings. Marla the Sea Faerie met with Tronot, and he knows our wisdom is powerful. Thankfully, Marla talked him out of nuking Lake Tahoe. He is afraid of our wisdom. He is right to be afraid! Fortunately, too, the Zoloatons have placed a force field around the Wisdom Palace that no nuclear device could ever penetrate.

"You have all learned that there are only two emotions in this world that generate physical vibrations in Earth's core and atmosphere: fear and love. All other feelings are offshoots of these two. All rage is fear. All greed is fear. All joy is love. Etcetera. Your severed spines are opened to the openings in the spine of Earth, so your emotions affect Earth far more deeply than unopened spines. It would take thousands of warriors to do what the eighteen of you can do, with your emotions felt strongly, harnessed, and focused.

"You will not enjoy the Fear Battles, and I'm sorry, but you have to learn clairvoyance, and you have to know your crew members' worst fears, as well as your enemies' worst fears. This knowledge could save your life. Our goal in this war is to shed not one single life, theirs or ours. Their goal is to kill us all. Pretty tough odds, but their weapons of mass destruction will seem silly against our Weapons of Light and The ancient Wisdom Within.

"Each of you will have a coach trained in the most ancient ways. Trust your coach completely, even though your lessons will cause you pain. Open yourselves to all things. We begin!"

We turned away from Ulena, and there, before us was Marla, the Sea Faerie Keeper of Memories. Oh, great, I got Marla as a coach, the Marla who hated me.

Marla floated before us in her jellyfishy body. She flared all red and firey. "I do not hate you, Pepper—not even remotely. Hate no longer exists for my race. For a time, I was jealous of you, and jealousy, I thought, was also an ancient emotion we'd never again know. As Ulena said, all emotion stems from fear or love. Queen Rona was so fond of you, I became afraid she would love me less. I was shocked to know I could feel such an old-fashioned emotion connected to the fear of losing Rona's love, but I did. I am sorry. In truth, I have been connected to your clan from the beginning, and my love for all of you has guided me down through the millennia. Nanu was as a daughter to me, as all the members of your clan have been my children, for me to guide, and watch, and protect. I love you, Pepper, more than I have realized before saying it aloud in this moment."

With those words, Marla showered me with a golden, loving light that felt warm and rich. I spread my arms wide so my heart could open and take in her love, and I felt all the ancestors of my clan with me in that amazing moment. Marla became sister and mother in my heart, in that moment.

I was so sick of everyone reading my thoughts, though! "You know, Marla, I'd love it if I could turn off my thoughts so everybody around here could give me some privacy in my head, once in awhile."

Marla smiled. She had returned to a blue-violet color. "Try not to think so loudly, Pepper."

I blushed, and everyone smiled. I felt like a total deufuss.

"Once you know and understand clairvoyance, you'll learn to turn the volume of your thoughts down, so they can't be read," Marla said. "Okay, everyone, get into a state of total relaxation, into a place within yourselves of deep and quiet calm. By now, you should be able to get there readily, using your breath techniques. Go there now.

"While in this trance state, decide firmly the one thing in life you are most afraid of, and think it loudly. Louder, Todd. I want you to visualize your greatest fear in huge black letters, on a giant billboard for all of us to read. Very good, Danu, and Pepper. Okay, Todd, that's good. Todd and Pepper, you have the same biggest fears. Stay in your deep calm state, but open your eyes and read each other's greatest fears."

I opened my eyes, still feeling woozy, and read Todd's "sign." It read: "I might never play hockey again," just as if it were a giant sign on a billboard on the side of the road. It was embarrassing, but he read mine: "I might never run for a touchdown pass again." Our greatest fears seemed so trite in the face of world domination by the Greed Kings, but there they were, big and trite, in black and white, for all the Champion Warriors of the Universe to read.

We looked around at the fears of the others. Tamdin's was, "I might fail at the mission my whole life has been about." Arinne's was more personal: "I am afraid of losing him again, too soon." Micah's was like Tamdin's, about possible failure in this mission, and Danu's was intensely personal and noble at the same time: "I might never bring children of my own into the new world of peace and compassion."

We closed our eyes, and Marla told the others to read each other's fears. Everyone was quiet; we were incredibly, nakedly vulnerable.

"You have to know this about each other if you are going to defend each other, and trust your lives to each other. You have to know the greatest fears and the greatest motivations of each member of your crew. We can talk about motivations now, because they are connected to greatest fears."

"Every time we find each other," said Arinne, holding Tamdin's hand, and looking into his eyes, "it is a time of chaos, and our souls have signed on to save and heal the world. Just once, I would like a long, quiet life with this soul I have loved so deeply, for so many eons. That is my inner motivation, beyond saving the world again."

In my whole life, I never saw anyone look at another person the way they looked at each other. The souls behind Arinne and Tamdin's eyes swallowed each other, and then dove back and forth, from Tamdin to Arinne and back. They breathed in unison, and they blinked in unison. I'm not the most romantic person in the world, but this knocked my socks off.

Tamdin said quietly, "For me, too."

"I would love to find a love like yours, someday," Danu said, "and bring children into a world of peace and compassion."

Micah said, "I want all Native people to live exactly as they want, in beauty, joy, and freedom, in their Mother Earth's arms."

Todd took my hand and laughed. He shouted, "Pepper and I just want to run and play! Marla, are we noble and big enough to be on this crew? Pepper and I look like the little kids on the block."

"Your hearts are much nobler and bigger than you know," she said, and smiled. Marla's love encircled us. "Very wise ones put the crews together. Both of you felt the simultaneous whoosh of love from a huge number of fans when you were hurt. That huge electrical surge of love transformed you forever. You would gladly die for any one of those fans who shot love into you that day. You've never met those fans, but you would die for them. You would certainly die for each other, without thinking. You have passion for your sports, and you love the surge of playing your games well. If that is enough to drive you for now, then I gladly hold the promise of hockey and football in your futures if we win this. I tell you also, you will find so much more, in this battle."

The others in our crew gazed at Todd and me as if we were adorable children. It did not take any clairvoyance skills to know that Danu and Tamdin had never seen a hockey stick in their lives. There probably aren't too many broadcasts of football in the rain forests and Tibetan Himalayas, either. But I clung to what Marla had said about our super-charged up hearts, because I knew that was true. I remembered the moment it happened: all the love surging through me as I lay there on the football field.

"You're going to practice clairvoyance, both reading the thoughts of others, and blocking your thoughts so they can't be read. When you get really good, you'll be able to read a Greed King's thoughts best when he is trying to block his thoughts."

"Are there no Greed Queens, Marla?" Arinne asked.

Marla smiled. "Yes, but you will not meet them. They send the men to kill. Most of the kings love their money and power more than their women and children, but not all of them. Some of them love, and you can reach through their greed and touch them with their love of love. The end of hate and war in this world will come about because of a few Greed Kings' love of love. Never forget that. In that way, it is the Greed Kings who know how to love who will be the ultimate saviors of your world. It is you who will guide them to their true hearts."

Marla shook her huge mane of inky black hair, as if to shake the thought of the Greed Kings from her shoulders. "Now, back to the lessons. Blocking your thoughts is a simple matter of not thinking so loudly when you are near clairvoyants. Danu, you, I believe, were taught by your people to practice both clairvoyance and blocking. Show them."

Danu smiled shyly. She said, "This is loud thinking," and her face blushed as we read her thoughts like a billboard in the air above her. "I wonder what is hockey?" All of us laughed.

"It's the coolest game on earth, Danu!" Todd told her.

She smiled. "Now, when you want to block your thoughts, you keep them down here," she said, and she pressed into her heart with a surprisingly strong fist. "You must focus on keeping your thoughts quiet, and centered in your heart."

"We can do this!" Todd cheered.

"Are you sure you were never a cheerleader?" I teased him.

"Can't remember ever looking good in skirts," he teased back.

"OK, Danu, see if you can read my quiet thoughts," Todd dared.

"Todd, I don't think you've ever done anything quietly, but okay, you try," Danu teased.

Todd, who loved it when everyone gave him center stage, shuffled in his chair. He took a deep breath, and tried to "think quietly."

We laughed and laughed. Most of his thoughts were blocked, except for one word. It was embarrassing and cool; the one word was "Pepper." I blushed. Everyone made whistling and "oooooh," sounds, but my face got red as a tomato.

"What?" Todd asked.

Tamdin whispered in Todd's ear what we'd seen. "Okay, so you know I like her," Todd said. "Duh! I covered up the rest of my thoughts, didn't I? I did pretty good for a first time, don't you think, Danu? Give me a break!'

Danu laughed. "Yes, Todd. You did well." When she giggled, Danu came to life as a pretty, gregarious young woman. Todd could do that for anyone, I decided. "Okay, everyone else, you think you're so great, now you try," Danu ordered, still giggling.

We had the giggles, and started throwing loud, funny thoughts in the air like little kids. "Brain Fart," "Fumble Breath," and equally dumb sayings started flashing in front of us, and it wasn't just Todd and me playing. "Monkey Poop" came from Danu's head, and "Rancid Sod" came from Arinne.

Marla was smiling and nodding approval. "There will be moments during the battle when you will need to flash your thoughts just so to each other. You are doing well, you silly Earth monkeys."

We settled down and focused, and thought quiet thoughts, pressing them into our hearts. We kept them in our hearts, and Marla and Danu couldn't read them. I was thrilled! Finally, I would be able to keep some thoughts to myself.

"We're doin' it, Marla!" Todd shouted.

A huge voice came booming into the hall. "Bravo, Mr. Hockey Puck!" We recognized Butara's Party DJ voice.

Marla laughed that splashy rainbow laugh all the Kobans do, and the air around us filled with colors and tinkling bell sounds. "You are magnificent, all of you!" she shouted. "Now, Butara is going to teach all of us not only how to become invisible, which Kobans already know, but how to make our surroundings invisible. That is something I've always wanted to know. Butara?" she called, swirling the colors in the air surrounding her as she whirled, looking for him. "You funny lizard, where are you?" She squealed, and laughed and laughed, while colors splashed all around us. An invisible Butara was tickling her jellyfish-feet things.

Butara became visible again. I'd forgotten how huge he was. Twelve feet tall is really tall! He towered over all of us, laughing heartily. Our eyes soared, up and up, past the glowing, golden clothes, past his white-gold, shining heart, and into his deeply glowing, amber eyes. He radiated pure joy and peace. With him in our presence, I could easily believe in a world of harmony and joy.

"Okay, Earth and Koban People. Whoa, look who's also showin' up! The Ancient Earth People, Lillith and Bromand. Welcome, everyone! Gather around."

I hadn't seen Lillith and Bromand since my first astral journey, which now seemed to be eons ago. They floated in the air, as if it were normal. (Well, I guess everything in the Wisdom Palace is normal!) They were magnificent, and beaming with happiness.

"We wish to watch, and take part," Lillith said, in her beautiful voice, and Marla went to embrace her.

"Mama! My mother! Oh, Mother, I've missed you!" Marla wept into her Lemurian mother's white robes. Her mother glowed with love as she held her daughter. Butara and the rest of us felt almost embarrassed, but it was so beautiful. We all had tears in our eyes.

Butara mimicked an embarrassed Earth person, and cleared his throat. We were all so happy! "Okay," Butara said, "the lesson is invisibility. I brought Lillith and Bromand here because they're good at this, and they're Earth people with Earthly belly buttons. You'll need those belly buttons!" He laughed.

Marla laughed her splashing, tinkling, rainbow-colored Koban laugh. She stepped aside so everyone could see Lillith's bare belly button. What toned tummy muscles she had, especially for a lady who was, like, thirteen thousand years old.

Marla sounded like a little girl as she said, "This is Lillith, my mother from Mu."

Butara said, "now while I talk, Lillith is going to demonstrate. It's easy as pie! Did you know they used to say that on Earth? I have no idea what it means, but it's a cute old Earth expression, and I've learned 'em all. Okay, everyone, use the Perfect Breath to get into a meditative state. One, two, three, you're there." His voice changed to its soothing tone of meditative direction. "Now, as you focus on your breathing from the diaphragm, I want you to imagine all of yourself emptying. Empty yourself of all thoughts. Empty yourself of all emotions, and empty yourself of all past thoughts, emotions, and experiences. That is very good, everyone. Now, I want you to imagine all thoughts, past events, emotions, and experiences are actually traveling through your belly button. Follow all your thoughts, past events, emotions, and experiences through your belly buttons, like a thread. Hold the thread, and feel your whole body thread through the belly button. Hold onto the thread, and vibrate with the only thing left of your being: your love and compassion. Voila! My, oh, my, what students you are! Congratulations, Crew! You are all invisible."

He cleared his throat dramatically. "You don't have to cheat, Pepper. You can open your eyes all the way, and look at the hockey dude. He's invisible, I tell you!"

"Wow!" I shouted. "Todd, you are totally invisible!"

I guess he opened his eyes, too. "So are you! This is so fun!"

The six of us were all invisible, and we played with it. We reached for each other, bumping arms and chairs, and laughing. Laughter broke the spell, and it was fun to watch each other become visible again. I think all of us were beginning to see how much power there was inside each one of us.

"You guys make me look good," Butara said. A happy, golden light illuminated his face and the crinkles around his eyes when he smiled widely down at us. "You learn fast. The next lesson is harder. It's about making your surroundings invisible. I live in a galaxy that was torn by war, eons ago, kinda like Earth was at the beginning of the twenty-first century. We didn't want to fight, or kill anybody, so we learned how to just make ourselves invisible. They can't kill what they can't see."

"You made an entire planet invisible?" Todd asked. His forehead wrinkled skeptically, and his head tilted. "I don't know, seems tough to believe."

"That's what we did, Hockey Man. Then we surrounded our invisible planet with an invisible, powerful force of love and compassion, like the one that is now surrounding the Wisdom Palace. Tronot's weapons cannot pierce the force we've put around the palace.

"We live a very peaceful life up there, on Zoloat. Don't ever let anybody tell you peace is dull, Earth people, because it is the most fun of anything."

Tamdin bent his head toward his chest, and raised his hand to his chin in a classic thinker's pose. "We are not advanced enough to do as you Zoloatons have. Even with the ancient wisdom, and remembering, I doubt we could make the entire Sun Quartz Fields invisible."

"No, I don't think you could, either," Butara interrupted.

Tamdin's chiseled, Asian face held us breathless. "Is it your intention to teach us to make our small, immediate surroundings invisible, such as the spacecraft we'll be using to approach the Sun Quartz Fields?"

"That's it, Mountain Man! They can't shoot what they can't see. And your spacecraft, besides being invisible, will be surrounded with a shield of Compassion, created by the Kobans and Zoloatons, together for the first time on this stage. You can't get much safer than that! Your planet is loved by Kobans and Zoloatons, and Kobans and Zoloatons agree: your time for the final world is now. Of course, we don't have the final-final say—that's for the Ultimate Prime Creator—but I think you got it going there, too."

"When do we meet the astronauts who'll do the actual flying of the ships?" Todd asked.

"You met one of 'em, right here," Butara said, pounding on his or her golden chest. "I get to fly the big ship, the one that'll be causin' all the trouble to old Tronot. I'll be invisible the whole time, but I'll be the sole controller of the cockpit that Marla—the supposed NASA astronaut—will pretend to manage."

"Cool," I said.

"Yeah, Baby, and Rakama will be flying Todd's ship. Other fabulous Zoloatons will drive the other ships. We are really good at flying spacecraft."

That meant everything, for just being in the Zoloatons' presence felt safe, and warm, and free.

PREPARING FOR BATTLE

From the Earth Memories Archives
Compiled by Pepper McCullah
Clan of the Fan-Feathered Brow
Earth Year 2030

Our other lessons were harder. Learning to make our surroundings invisible took the crew a week of ten-hour days. Making a rock invisible was easy for Micah and Tamdin, because they could find the spirit inside the rock, and talk to it, and make it vibrate until it became invisible. Wheelchairs and rocket-ships' spirits are not so easy to talk to! Butara was patient, explaining that we would speak to the spirit of the heart of the person who made the rocket ship and the wheelchair.

"All things come from spirit," Butara said. "Find the spirit, and communicate."

Working with the advanced breathwork techniques we'd studied—the ones that had been handed down to humans for seventy millennia—we finally were able to communicate with the spirit left by those who made the rockets and the wheelchairs.

I wanted to slap somebody, I was so dizzy with joy the first time I made myself and my wheelchair disappear!

"Pepper! You're doin' it! You and the chair are invisible! Congratulations!" Todd hollered.

We were jubilant, as one by one the six warriors of our crew vanished from sight. Six invisible chairs with six invisible warriors floated about twelve feet above the ground. We cruised just above Butara's bald, golden head, laughing and singing! It ranked right up there among the happiest days of our lives. Butara, Ulena, and Marla levitated with joy and love and laughter for us, their wheelchair warrior students.

Butara told us we would be spending the next week perfecting our skill, because making the wheelchair we lived in vanish was much easier than making two rocket-ships invisible.

"Get it down, this week, and then you won't believe how easy it is to make a giant rocket ship disappear," Butara told us.

When we had our invisibility skills perfected, we were taken to the rocket-ship launching center. Ulena explained the actual flight plans of the ships, and who would fly what. That was when I learned how dangerous my mission would be.

"Marla will be flying the ship with Tronot. His money has bought the finest nuclear-and fuel-cell-powered spacecraft, so we plan to take advantage, and hitch a ride," Ulena said. "Pepper will be in the cockpit with Marla."

Gad! "Ulena, are you serious? I am going to be in the cockpit with the most evil guy of all time?"

Ulena smiled. "The bravest ones are those who admit their fears and conquer them. You will be spectacular, Pepper, and everyone in your crew knows it. They voted for you."

I looked around at my crew in disbelief. "You <u>did</u>?"

They nodded. "Pepper, you are so brave," Danu said softly.

"Why don't I know it?"

"You're simply used to being you," Arinne said. "You take your tremendous power and boldness for granted. Pepper McCullah, you were our only choice. It was unanimous."

"Thank you for your faith in me," I mumbled. "I'll try not to let you down."

"Failure isn't an option, Beautiful. You're gonna kick butt," Todd said. "Can we talk about me, now?"

Everyone laughed.

Todd shifted excitedly in his chair, and waved his arms while he spoke. "Pepper, I get to use my hockey stick, and whack the Zombie Ghouls right smack into the Sun Quartz Fields, just as the Equinox gets ready to fire up the Fields."

"Ulena, can you explain the whole deal about the Zombie Ghouls?" I asked. "I was in Koba, that day, meeting Queen Rona."

"Yes. Zombie Ghouls are mutants who were ruined by the acids and gaseous toxins from Gonaquadet's explosion. The Zombie Ghouls have tremendous energy, but they live in sadness that they drown with addictions. Their terrible negativity poisons both Earth and the cosmos. Todd is going to free them, from both their sadness and their addictions. Their tremendous negative energy will be transformed into the vast energy of eternal joy as they live within the Sun Quartz Fields. Their destiny as the new Light Beings is beautiful."

"Cool," I said. "And Tronot—my job is to do what with him?"

"Your job is to stay alive, Pepper. When Tronot discovers his massive transfer hoses have been slashed by a certain, naughty Zoloaton, he will go quite berserk. You will face grave danger. Stay alive, and use your heart. Use everything you've learned, and use his weakness and his strength to set him free from evil forever."

I trembled. The faces of Arinne, Danu, Micah, Tamdin, and Todd were filled with compassion; they knew I was terrified. They read my thoughts, and they read my face. I could also read their thoughts and feelings of love and belief. I was honored. Terrified, but honored.

"I will do my very best," I said.

A slight shadow of worry darkened Todd's sunny face for just a moment, but he gave me his cheerleader routine, anyway. "You will be magnificent!"

"You will triumph, for all humankind," Tamdin said softly.

Ulena wanted to continue her battle-plan briefing. "Tamdin, Arinne, Micah, and Danu will be in one ship. You will combine your powers to make your ship invisible. Rakama is your captain. Danu, no matter what chaos surrounds you, you must play your flute until your most ancient DNA tells you the ancient song the Light Beings sang. Deep within the quartz fields, they will hear, and waken, and sing with your flute. Arinne, the memories of your many ancestor priestesses are lying dormant in your DNA. When Danu's music wakens the Light Beings, you will be jolted with enough electrical energy to kill an ordinary mortal. You will whisper the memories and ancient tales the Light Beings heard before entering the Sleep of Bliss. You will give the signal; there will be no doubt when it is time for Micah and Tamdin to find the exact spots within the Sun Quartz Fields that are open to communication. With your open hearts, Micah and Tamdin, you will speak to them, and convince them to ignite for all humankind. You must convince them Earth is ready.

"The ancient memories lying dormant in Todd's DNA will also awaken at that moment, and he will shout the ancient formula buried in the language of his ancestors' runes. He will babble while Danu plays her flute in a more and more frenzied tone. His intonations and Danu's flute will be loudly heard through speakers in all your ships, and the speakers will project your song and your chants and your memories all over the cosmos. When this happens, we will all know, the equinox is near.

"At the exact moment of equinox, we will all be united in spirit, mind, heart, and soul, and you will experience the New Dawn, spoken of through all the ages. Our hearts, bodies, minds, and souls will be united with all things, throughout the universe." Ulena smiled, and spoke almost to herself. "It will feel good, to be free."

"Ulena, what if it doesn't work? I mean, I hate to be a downer, but I want to know," I said.

"Earth will hobble along until it ends, sad and broken. I don't believe that is our destiny, Pepper.

"Now, I want all of you to go to your families tonight, and love them. You will soon be in space, and some of you may not return."

Ulena motioned to our families, who were crowded just outside the crystal doors leading to the Golden Domed Athlete's Hall.

We watched our families enter the Golden Domed Athlete's Hall to retrieve us, for what might be our last days together. Tamdin's Tibetan family entered first, with their gentle, Asian faces shining. They were dressed in native, colorful, Tibetan robes: high collars, long sleeves, and pink, yellow, and blue and green stripes. Tamdin's parents beamed with pride as they approached their son. Micah's family looked familiar, because his parents and his brother and sister were all famous, Hopi-Navajo artists; I'd seen their work and their faces in magazines. I could my beloved Grandma Noni in all her descendants, and for a moment, I closed my eyes and felt her warmth. Danu's Mayan relations had beautiful Mayan faces, just as Arinne's Irish relatives all shared her Irish Sea-blue eyes. Poignantly, Arinne's family members surrounded Tamdin's family, in one massive hug. The hall was filled with their very ancient love-ties.

I was especially interested in Todd's relatives, because I knew his ancestry could be traced back to Mu. Also, okay, because I liked him a ton, and maybe I wanted to see who my future in-laws might be! They all looked like Todd: blonde, big-boned, and tall. They were athletic, strong, and proud of their Todd.

His mother, Freta, took my hand. Her sharp eyes fixed on mine.

"It is so good to finally meet you, Pepper McCullah," she said simply, looking into my heart. Her love was ferocious—a wild, Northern force.

Todd was thrilled when my famous quarterback dad entered the hall, and I felt glad to have such a handsome father. Collin and Sol entered just behind him; they looked so much like my father. Why had I never noticed it, before?

It felt like a big party, but when my famous mother entered the Hall, everyone stopped talking and became reverent. She nodded at everyone—some people, including Ulena, bowed when she passed—and I was dazzled. My graceful, beautiful mother—healer, scientist, and Earth Core Tunnel Mother—had brought us to this pivotal point in Earth's destiny. She had studied the ancient wisdom texts passed down from her ancestor, Nanu, and had made sense of them. She'd understood the words in the texts that had led her to the Sun Quartz Fields, and their secrets, their promise.

Dad was joking with Todd when Mom approached, and I just had to love him for the way he looked at her. They'd survived what was nearly the end of Earth, and their love would survive to celebrate the beginning of the New Dawn.

Mom kissed my forehead. "How do you feel?"

"Scared," I said.

Mom smiled. "Good. Let's go home."

Danu's tiny mother with the strong Mayan features approached us. "We would like to have a party in the hall, with dancing and music. Danu's brothers and sisters are all fine musicians, and would like to celebrate once, together, all the Clans of Light, with our Warriors."

A huge, booming voice sounded above our heads that was unmistakably Zoloatonian. "Sounds good to us! We love parties!"

Before the astonished eyes of our families, two of our twelve-foot tall, Zoloaton teachers materialized. Butara and Rakama were holding huge, beautiful, ancient-looking drums with cymbals on them.

Recovering from their shock, Danu's relatives started to play lively dancing music. Butara and Rakama drummed an ancient, haunting beat that had all our feet and hands tapping. Jim scooped up Alaiya in his arms, and they began to dance and swirl across the marble floor. Ulena's head swayed, and she smiled happily. Various brothers and sisters from each of the clans approached members of the other clans to dance. I felt so happy, I could have popped.

Todd took my hand, and suggested we swirl around in our chairs to the music. We did so, laughing and twirling our heads off. It was at the end of a very lively song, when I was almost completely out of breath, that he kissed me for the first time. I will never forget that kiss! It was big and sloppy and warm.

MY VISIT WITH CALEINA AND THE MOTHER IBIS

From the Earth Memories Archives
Compiled by Pepper McCullah
Clan of the Fan-Feathered Brow
Earth Year 2030

Magically, tables filled with food and punch appeared. We laughed, and feasted, and danced, and sang. It was long after midnight before the warriors and their families went home, with love and laughter and music in their hearts.

Still laughing, I felt flushed in the crisp, Sierra mountain air as we got into our car. The party had been wonderful! How I wished I'd had a camera, and photographed Sol's face when he first laid eyes on Butara and Rakama. My family had loved watching us do invisibility tricks. It'd been good practice.

We sang some of the songs Danu's family had taught us, during the ride to our house. I felt, strangely, identically as I used to feel before my family and I would pile into the car for one of my football games. I felt my brothers' pride, and complete faith in my abilities, once as a football player and now as a Wisdom Retriever. It was good to be loved by this beautiful family! I would not let them down.

Mom sat by my bed and stroked my hair as she used to when I was little. "Don't be afraid, my darling girl. All your clan is with you, and you will meet them very soon." Her green eyes were shining with secret knowledge.

Almost two in the morning when she left my bedside, I went into that instant, sweet, deep sleep we only know when we are certain we are well loved.

I was jolted instantly awake, as if someone had turned on an electric switch in me. I looked at the clock, which said three a.m., and my eyes focused on a small orb of white-greenish light that spun swiftly in a circle. The glowing orb's diameter was growing constantly as it approached my bed.

The orb became a large ibis with snow-white wings that stretched across my entire room. She was so beautiful! I'd heard about this magical bird who'd loved and rescued my ancestors down through the millennia, and my heart opened in love and wonder. Her deep eyes were kind, and sweet. I heard and felt her speak to me in my head.

"I will be with you, and the spirits of your ancestors—your clan—will be with you in that ship. You are right to be afraid, but you will not be alone." Warmth from her fluttering, beautiful wings kissed my face. She stepped backward as another spinning, glowing orb of green light appeared in front of her.

The orb became a giant owl. I knew from my ancestors' stories it was Caleina, who'd once told Nanu about the future of her clan on this continent. Caleina was not so motherly and warm as the mother ibis; her eyes burned fiercely into mine. The brows above her eyes knitted together, and when she spread her wings, a cold, strong wind shook the room. My heart pounded. Staring deeply into the hypnotic swirls of brown, gray, white, and black patterns in her feathers, I felt her power. Filled with millennia-worth of wisdom, she now transferred jolts of her surging strength to me. Her love was ferocious and silent. I felt a swelling shift: from feeling tiny and frightened, my breath changed, until I felt like a balloon, growing and rising. Limitless strength now raged in me. Finally, she communicated.

"You have been well chosen."

With that, she vanished. In my room, where the ancient mother ibis and Caleina had once stood, there now appeared spirits, beginning with the Laughing Lady, Re-ve, and her horse, Shima.

"Make us proud, old girl! My feisty spirit and the spirit of my Shima go with you to battle." The vision of them softly evaporated.

Nanu appeared briefly. "I will be with you in the ship, dear Pepper."

Grandma Noni briefly appeared. "*Tsilkali*, Little Bird, fly true."

A fragrant pink flower filled the space where the spirits had been, but the spirits were gone. I felt honored and loved, by millennia worth of clan members. My destiny awaited me.

"Bring it on!" I shouted.

THE BATTLE BEGINS

From the Earth Memories Archives
Compiled by Pepper McCullah
Clan of the Fan-Feathered Brow
Earth Year 2030

I slept sweetly, yet was startled to find Marla sitting on my bed when I woke. Dressed in her beautiful, purplish-blue, jellyfishy form, her beautiful, dark eyes were soft and loving. I could see she was thinking about all the millennia she'd spent, preparing my clan for this day. (How about that? It was getting so I could read other people's thoughts, for a change.)

"Nice work, reading my mind, Pepper McCullah. You are right: it all comes down to this day. I am filled with love and honor, to have served the Clan of the Fan-Feathered Brow. Are you ready to do battle?"

"Absolutely."

"Let's go. I will be taking an Earth form, and I want you to see my form now, so you don't laugh at the wrong time in front of Tronot."

Marla waved her jellyfish arm, which was like a violet, liquid-lacy sleeve, until she was completely transformed. I gasped. She looked like Nanu! And me! She had the same feathery eyebrows, which arched above her rich, dark eyes.

"I'm glad you warned me. Did you freak his DNA memory, or what?"

"Oh, yes I did. I worked with that nagging DNA memory of his, and you will see me doing so, our entire time together. As you could be my little sister, you will also be tweaking him, to use one of your words. Our knowledge of his nastiest life gives us power."

While Marla and I sat together, chatting, my heart swelled with love for my entire clan, and for all of my history. I loved Koba and Zoloat's Enlightened Ones, for loving us enough to guide us to this moment.

There were details, however, nagging at me, and in this intimate moment, I pressed to understand. Raising myself onto one elbow, I asked, "Marla, how could he kill Nanu, if he loved her so much?"

"I asked myself that very question, as I transcribed everything. He obviously didn't love her. He desired her, and he hated himself for desiring anything except power. So he really hated her." She laughed that Koban laugh that sends colors and tinkling bells into our Earth air. "Pepper, I've been in human form, for several lives, and I still don't really understand humans very well." She laughed again. My room was swirling with colors: turquoise, hot pink, orange, and purple.

"You know, I don't think it's a good idea to do any laughing on Tronot's ship. The rainbow laughs kind of give you away," I reminded her.

Queen Rona instantly floated above the floor of my room. "Please, Marla, you funny girl," she said, and her tinkling laughter-rainbow swirled with the leftover colors of Marla's.

"Pepper, and Marla, I love you with my whole heart, and I am very, very proud of you. Vaya con Dios," she said, ("go with God," in modern Spanish, as well as in many, ancient languages). She then vanished as swiftly as she'd appeared.

"To the battlefield, then, my warrior!" Marla ordered, and we were off as soon as I could get dressed and hug my family goodbye.

For my brothers, the hugs were brisk, slap-on-the-back affairs, for they were certain I'd return triumphant. Hugging my dad was painful, for he cried and cried. Mom was braver, but no less worried. I held her hand. I had with me the tiny pouch of earth from Lake Tahoe's shore she'd given me long ago, before Gonaquadet. I lifted it to my heart and held it there. Just as she reported I said before we went below, into the Earth Core Tunnels, when I was two, I said to her, "It'll be okay, Mom. I'll come home."

My hands were sweaty as I wheeled myself before Tronot. He resembled Memsek too closely for my comfort. He had Memsek's dark, thick eyebrows, and his black eyes held no warmth. One eyebrow raised when he saw me, and he spoke to Marla, who was now Nora Whitely, the famous astronaut.

"Nora, I don't remember you mentioning you'd be bringing your crippled little sister aboard. She is your sister, isn't she?"

He so gave me the creeps, staring at my fan-feathered brow the way he did! I shuddered, and thought to myself the old adage, "do the crime, do the time." In Memsek's case, a crime he committed over six thousand years ago still haunted him.

Marla stood silent for a brief moment, and I knew she was working his brain telepathically. Gosh, she was good!

"Mr. Tronot, this is Pepper McCullah, my famous cousin. She was a football player: the most valuable player in the '29 Superbowl. Since her unfortunate accident, surely you remember her extraordinary work with me at NASA. She will be invaluable on our mission! Surely you have also read the data suggesting that breaks in the spine open humans to communication with all minerals." Most of what Marla had said was true, except I'd never set foot on NASA grounds as anything but a tourist.

"Oh, yeah! Well, okay," was all he could say.

Once inside our space suits, we entered the cockpit. I was shaking all over, until I felt a familiar warmth and peace surround me. Butara was invisible, here, inside the cockpit! I breathed in the ancient way, connecting my heart to that of the big, golden space lizard. Careful not to audibly sigh, I surrendered to a complete bliss sweeping over me.

Being in a space ship was wondrous. Space travel had become commonplace for the very wealthy, even before Gonaquadet, and then after the cataclysm, governments sent nuclear-powered shuttles into space to monitor, and search, for any other wayward comets or asteroids. The Greed Kings relied heavily on space travel for profit. They'd built a vast empire, crushing vast space rocks and using the big, volatile energy they supplied to power their empire.

Because time was so different now from the way it had been before Gonaquadet, and because ships moved on speedy light laser paths beamed from Earth, it no longer took lengthy trips to reach distant planets. We would reach the Sun Quartz Fields in two days, even though they were five million miles from Earth. Our plan was to arrive at the Sun Quartz Fields on December 21st, so we'd have all of December 22nd to plan the exact Equinox moment for harnessing the power.

I envied the other members of my crew, for they were free to be their real selves, and talk about their true missions. I had to pretend I was helping the Greed Kings steal the power from the Light Beings, so they could gouge people on Earth. They wanted to recycle the old, dark ages of the twenty-first century before Gonaquadet, where the rich milked the poor to become obscenely richer, and the poor became more destitute.

My heart was with Todd, who by now was heading for the Zombie Ghouls' Station in space. The International Space Station had once been a place inhabited by noble astronauts from all over the world who worked together, studying ways to better life on Earth. Now, lonely mutant Zombie Ghouls spent their time on the Station zapping Earth with negativity and addiction energy. Todd's mission was to use a stick the Kobans had affectionately shaped like a hockey stick, in Todd's honor. The magical stick was filled with the same, glowing power Nanu and Makara had used to heal, in ancient times, and Todd would use it to whack the Zombie Ghouls right into the Sun Quartz Fields. The miserable ghouls would be transformed into bliss-filled Light Beings who would help power the New Dawn with their loving light. After the New Dawn, the Space Station would again be used for the good of all the universe.

The glowing energy crystals now implanted in the hockey stick had been in storage, with their energy dormant, beneath the rear paws of the Sphinx at Giza for over ten thousand years. When the Sphinx had imploded, the crystals' energy had magically come alive again, ever-growing, until now the crystals were as powerful as they'd been in Atlantis over 10,000 years ago. This hockey stick was ready for some serious work!

By the time the whacked and flying ghouls reached the Fields, Todd would be shouting the ancient, sacred chants from the runes that would ignite them. This was our elaborate plan. I had as much faith in Todd as he had in me. His ancient lineage went back as far as mine, and I could imagine his ship filled with spirits from Mu, and ancient Scandinavia. Lillith herself, the Mother of Mu—Motherland of the Lotus—would be flying with him. She was one, tough figurehead! He would not fail with Lillith in his ship.

A million things could go wrong, but when I began to worry, I felt Butara's huge, golden hand above my head. He/she was scrubbing over my worrisome thoughts with peace, love, and massive faith.

WE REACH THE SUN QUARTZ FIELDS

From the Earth Memories Archives
Compiled by Pepper McCullah
Clan of the Fan-Feathered Brow
Earth Year 2030

Space travel was unreal. Liftoff was like the biggest surging jolt of a rush! It felt like my face was going to melt off. Once we blasted through Earth's atmosphere, though, it was pretty floaty. The ship never felt as if it was moving that much. I couldn't help but wax poetic while I gazed at Earth, far below. She was pretty banged up from Gonaquadet, but she still quite beautiful. She looked blue, with white, swirly clouds encircling her, and peppered with small, jagged brown patches of land where there used to be huge continents. I tried to find Lake Tahoe, and thought about my parents, who were probably at this moment looking at the sky through the giant telescope at the Wisdom Palace Observatory. They were trying to spot me, and chart my progress. I felt their love.

Nothing looks like the universe of stars as you travel among them in space. Nothing like passing the giant, ivory-colored orb of Earth's moon, or approaching the vivid, golden crescent of Venus. Our point of destiny, the Sun Quartz Fields, was 5 million miles into space from home. Venus, of course, was about 8 million miles from home, but Venus has always shone brightly from the shores of Lake

Tahoe! From the sky, she was a vivid, molten gold: golder than the brightest day. The sun's brilliance, the closer we got to Venus, was blinding. Because Venus was so much closer to the sun than Earth, her surface was hot as boiling oil, consistently about 860 degrees Fahrenheidt, or 460 degrees Celsius. She looked that hot!

On our long journey into space, I found myself with time to work on these memories archives, with Marla guiding me telepathically. Marla told Tronot I was charting our course when he asked. She had to spend a lot of time conferring with him about the details: what would happen at Equinox, and how they'd hook up the hoses (I felt Butara chuckle at that). I didn't envy her; Tronot had this nasty snarl when he talked.

What I found most frightening about Tronot was his casual attitude toward torture and killing. His conscience was immune to the idea that killing was bad; people who got in his way would be eliminated with the absent-minded ease one used to clean their fingernails of unwanted debris. Marla asked, once, what would happen if they met with Wisdom Retriever ships in a certain, delicate area.

He casually answered, "We'll kill them, of course."

I don't remember exactly when on the trip we spotted the Sun Quartz Fields; I only remember the light, and will remember that first light, for as long as I live. Our entire space ship had two of the tiniest windows, yet all of a sudden, the inside of our ship was fully bathed in heavy, pink light. It was magical! Everyone's faces shone with rosy light. And these Sun Quartz Fields were dormant! What would it be like when they ignited?

Legend songs my mother had learned from Koba sang that the Sun Quartz Fields were made of tears cried by God and the angels while witnessing the vast cataclysms on Earth down through the eons—a vast span, millions of years. These holy tears had filled with Light Beings who'd agreed to sleep in bliss within the fields until Earth was ready for a life without suffering.

The Sun Quartz Fields stretched as far as we could see. They were half as big as the entire planet of Venus! (Venus is roughly the same size as Earth.) They truly looked like pink teardrops that had melted, then flash frozen. Their pink light was blinding. Each new acre of quartz was totally different from the last—like snowflakes, or grains of sand beneath a microscope. Truly, like tears. How could so many wondrous shapes and different designs possibly exist?

I was distracted from my awed gazing by chuckling in my head. I jolted in my seat when I heard Butara's voice shout inside my head, "Now comes some real mischief, Football Girl! Hang onto your hat!"

My whole nervous system zapped with an electrical charge of fear, as I sensed Butara's invisible form was heading for the belly of the ship where the transfer system was stored.

"You and your crew just keep watching those pretty fields while I slash these babies," Butara's voice rang telepathically in my head.

Marla smiled at me warmly. She saw me tremble. "Do not be afraid," she told me telepathically. "Tronot cannot blame us. We have been up here, beneath his odious scrutiny, the entire flight. Do the ancient breathing, Pepper McCullah. Your time of battle approaches."

I went through each of my seven chakras, cleansing with breath in the ancient way. With the ancient breaths, I took my entire being, body, mind, heart and soul, into Peaceful Warrior Mode.

I was deep in a trance when Ganymede's torque jolted the ship. We were tossed on a wave of pure, surging force, like a rowboat in a big hurricane. Equinox was approaching! All of my DNA's memory chambers were flooding me with ancient wisdom. Fibers and cells in every part of me hummed with purpose, and I knew nothing else except this humming. The humming grew louder and louder until I finally surrendered, and dove into the humming sound. I guess I passed out; I remember nothing after that.

OUTSIDE THE GREED KINGS' SHIP

From the Earth Memories Archives,
Compiled by Marla, Sea Faerie
Keeper of Memories

Our ship is being tossed in the whirl of Ganymede's torque. I must will the words from my head into the archives, as physical writing is impossible. While Pepper's form fills with ancient knowledge and power activated within her DNA by the ancestors of her Clan, I have attuned myself to events outside the Greed Kings' ship. I must make sure all is going according to the elaborate plan mapped out through the ages.

Todd, the representative of the Clan of the Frozen Fields, is traveling in one, invisible ship. Rakama is pilot of the ship, and my own mother, Lillith, guides the ship well. Todd, clan bearer of the ancient runes, has blasted the Zombie Ghouls Station with his quartz-ignited stick. I see the ghouls flying by my tiny windows. They are smiling, and they are soaring blissfully toward the center of the Sun Quartz Fields, right on time.

In another ship, Clan Beyond the Mists' Arinne, Clan of Rock and Sun's Micah, Clan of the Highest Peaks' Tamdin, and Clan of the Forests' Danu sit in trances, while their clans' memories and powers are activated within their DNA. The Zoloat Buka pilots their ship perfectly. Bromand of Atlantis guides them well toward the heart of the fields.

The two invisible ships approach each other in the torque's chaotic whirl. I sense no fear coming from the Clans of Light, even though it appears they will collide. They have been trained well. Rakama steers the ship forcefully to avoid collision. Butara has succeeded in his most important mission: thwarting the Greed Kings' plan to harness the Sun Quartz Fields' power. He has gleefully slashed all the hoses, and shut down the harnessing engine for good. He is giggling and whooping so loudly, I can barely record. This giant, transcended master who in looks resembles a vast golden lizard, behaves more like an Earth monkey!

Pepper and the others from the Clans of Light are awakening from their deep trances. It is almost time. My entire being is suffused with rosy light from the wakening Sun Quartz Fields. I pulse with utter joy. Thirteen millennia worth of destiny awaits me; I surrender myself to the good of all: all humanity, and all beings throughout the universe. To feel this kind of love for all Creation was worth the many years and trials.

Pepper, I have come to know you, as I have come to know all bearers of the fan-feathered brow. I believe in you, and I love you with all my heart. My spirit soars with you, Caleina, Nanu, and Mother Ibis as you approach your great destiny.

THE FINAL BATTLE

From the Earth Memories Archives
Compiled by Pepper McCullah,
Clan of the Fan Feathered Brow
Earth Year 2031

I felt woozy, as if waking from a ten thousand year sleep. It had been a magical sleep. I dreamed of Makara, the healing priestess in Atlantis; she filled me with her healing powers. I dreamed of Nanu, who spoke to me of the ancient wisdom deep within myself. She performed the ancient ceremony in the dirt; she drew symbols in the dirt and threw dried reeds upon the symbols. A firepuff erupted, and briefly, a dazzling pink and golden light flashed before me. Nanu vanished. I then dreamed of my grandmother Meena from India, who told me I was her daughter that was never born into the world. I died in her womb, which was hot with typhus, she told me. We died together, and she has loved me. She is proud of me.

Next in my DNA reactivation trance rose Caleina; blue volts surged from her claws. Electric currents jolted through me, and she filled me with owl wisdom, and owl spirituality. Her golden eyes seared into me fiercely, so I trembled, even in my dream, but then I felt strong and brave.

I shook my head, and tried to remember my last conscious moments before the DNA reactivating trance began. I remembered the terrible shaking of the ship when we went through a major torque whirl from Jupiter's biggest moon, Ganymede. That was one fierce quake! Then I went into this trance. Now I felt ancient, and wise with vast knowledge. I felt connected to all my ancestors, and all living things. I felt total love for everyone who ever lived! It was a rush! It would have been nice to just sit and bliss out.

I could feel Todd speaking to me telepathically from his invisible ship, and I smiled. "If I don't make it," he said in my head, "can we meet again in another life, in a scene that blows everyone away, like when Tamdin and Arinne found each other again?"

"You'll make it, Todd. I want to do <u>this</u> life with you," I said into his head. "You are my destiny."

"I know. Wow, I'm filling up with all this weird rune language in my head! Get ready for Tronot to lose it a little. My speakers are cranked. Won't it be awesome, to have this rune chant come from out of nowhere? Pepper, I'm scared. Is my ship still completely invisible?"

"It absolutely is! Todd, you can do this."

Gorgeous, loud flute music suddenly filled our ship. Inside the ship and outside, Danu played a kind of flute music like no music I'd ever heard, accompanied by a big drumming to which the entire universe pulsed outside our ship. The very stars throbbed to the beat. Marla and I watched excitedly as the Sun Quartz Fields pulsed in rhythm. With every pulse, the fields grew brighter. The haunting music sounded South American and Native American. My skin prickled and felt alive. While the music played, I envisioned forests and rocks and sun and mountains. I felt peace.

Todd's voice loudly boomed along with the loud music, all through our ship. He spoke a strange, ancient language from the lands of ice. "*Uth na odin ger frern archt briern trn Frir grn trchnar-cht!!!*" He shouted. His voice was strange, and our ship shook to his booming, resonant intonations.

"What the hell is going on?" Tronot shouted.

Before Marla or I could make up a lie, a loud, panicky announcement from one of Tronot's other ships competed with the singing coming from the loudspeakers.

"Tronot! This is the captain of Omnipotence 3. We're feeling draft from three other ships out here. Invisible ships, Captain. Radar shows nothing, but they're here. Orders, sir?"

"Blast 'em, dammit!"

"Yes, sir, but it's hard to blast what you can't see, Captain."

"Blast everywhere around the drafts, Idiot! Get the other shooting ships, and blast their invisible asses to smithereens."

My gut froze. The Clans of Light, my grandparents, and Todd's parents were in those ships! A missile surged from one of Tronot's ships. I couldn't see our ships, of course—nothing had blown up yet, but I thought I would die of anxiety.

"Nora! This is the psycho fairies, I know it! We're gonna nuke 'em!"

Marla's voice took on an edge of power that shook everyone to attention, as if she'd grabbed all of us by the shirts. "Are you mad? You upset this atmosphere with too much blasting, and the Equinox emergence of the Sun Quartz Fields will never happen! They will remain pretty rocks in the sky, utterly lifeless for another million years. Stop your play games this instant, or this whole trip and your billions of dollars will be for nothing!"

When you study mastery for thirteen millennia, the way Marla has, you get really good. Old Tronot backed down quickly. "Captains, Ships Two and Three. Stop your fire!" Tronot yelled into his speaker.

He turned to Nora. His face was crazy red. "What are they doing out here?"

"Maybe they just want to watch the greatest cosmic event of all the ages," she said coolly.

"Nobody is going to take this from me! I need to destroy anything that stands in my way."

"They come in peace, not to take anything from you."

"You knew they were coming!"

"I couldn't imagine them <u>not</u> coming." Marla was hypnotizing him with her voice. I was having trouble staying awake. "This day has been foretold, Tronot, for seventy thousand years, down through all the ages. Nothing you do can stop this universe from changing, just as nothing could stop Gonaquadet…"

Marla droned on and on. It was really weird. All of Tronot's crew was falling into a trance, and her speakers were on, so I knew she was doing it to the crews in Tronot's other ships, as well. I clutched my stomach; I was terrified the Clans of Light crew would fall asleep and crash.

Butara's soothing voice in my head said, "She's good, isn't she, football girl? Don't you fall asleep, now. And don't you worry. Your hockey dude and the others are safe. The Greed Kings nicked your grandparents' ship, but Zoloatons are repairing the damage. The show must go on."

I smiled, and started to relax, although I knew the trance would not last long. Throughout the commotion, and despite having their ship fired at, Danu and Todd had not stopped their music and their chanting. The Sun Quartz Fields continued to pulse with every beat, growing dizzyingly bright and alive.

Tronot woke from his trance, and shouted to Marla. "Nora! It's about to happen, isn't it?"

"We're very close."

He turned to his crewmember in the cabin who was still woozy from the trance. He shouted. "Don't just stand there like a ninny! Get the hoses out there!"

"That won't be too easy, Dude," came Butara's booming, telepathic voice from the ceiling of our ship. Butara giggled at Tronot's horrified face when Tronot looked up toward Butara's invisible form. I was so sick with tension, I needed to heave.

Tronot got on the intercom. "Harness room: Activate the machines. Get the hoses out there and set them up. We are very near countdown."

Terror filled my gut, and my whole body shook. No magic breathing could keep me from dry heaving a little, for Tronot would discover the slashed hoses and the ruined harness machines. I wretched, but nothing came up, so I did the ancient, Perfect Breath to steady myself. I may soon be dead, but I would die sane.

Tronot's rage erupted throughout the ship, along with some swearing I had never even heard in football locker rooms. Tronot was in my face with a big fat gun. An assistant of his lunged at me from behind with another big gun. Behind me stood a guy with a big knife. I maneuvered in my chair the best I could, but it was a pretty feeble move.

Tronot cocked the big gun and I wheeled slightly away. The knife behind me stabbed into the back of my shoulder, all the way through my space suit.

"Tell me what's happening!" He shouted at me, purple with rage.

Marla jumped in front of my chair and pushed Tronot hard. The gun fired, hitting her in the abdomen. She fell. I reached for her from my chair, tears burning down my face. I was able to break her fall a little.

"Hold me so I can see," she said. She strained her neck toward the flashing, pulsing light outside our windows, and her eyes widened to take in all they possibly could. All she cared about was witnessing the New Dawn.

Without a second thought about Marla, Tronot raced frantically down to the Harness Room to see if he could salvage his plan. We could hear his shouting at the other ships to get their harness gear in place.

I lifted Marla onto my chair so she could see out the window. It was almost too bright. The music and the rune-language chant grew louder and louder, and we watched with glee as the Zombie Ghouls hit the heart of the Sun Quartz Fields. The moment each Ghoul hit, we could feel their joy. Our entire ship filled with the Zombie Ghouls' joy and freedom. Marla squeezed my hand feebly. She was losing her strength, and didn't have too much time. The glorious music was so loud, I think it gave her the power to hold on.

"Marla, hang on! We're almost there!" I whispered.

Tamdin's, Micah's, and Arinne's voices sang ancient songs in different languages. It was the most beautiful choir I'd ever heard, and their different languages blended magnificently with each other. Danu's flute twirled and rose among the singing and Todd's booming rune chants. A celestial concert, the entire heavens blazed with life. Each star grew brighter and brighter in the growing, throbbing pink light.

The Awakening will live in my DNA forever, and the memory will be passed down through the Clan of the Fan-Feathered Brow for all time. A massive explosion of pinkish-purplish light, followed by a blinding white flash, shook our ship. The explosion sent our ship reeling. When we could again see out the window, beautiful spirit beings flew into the air joyously. The Light Beings! Golden, dancing beings, they sang, in all languages, with the most glorious voices of all time. Their singing made us cry. Layers of pain and sadness lifted from our hearts. We began to sing with them in ten different, ancient languages. Marla sang the ancient words she remembered, in a beautiful, strong voice, somehow.

Another white-purple-pinkish blast erupted, and my body exploded from the wheelchair as I held Marla to me. Her face had lost all tension from her pain, and now shone with rapture. When I recovered from the blast, I was holding Marla in my arms, and standing on two solid, healthy legs. I could barely see, the light was so dazzlingly bright. Gently, I lay Marla, with her face toward the Sun Quartz Fields, in my wheelchair.

I felt Caleina near me. Owl-wisdom flooded my head as my fierce owl-gaze seared into Tronot's brain. Burning my owl-eyes into his head, I read his thoughts, and knew this was the moment Ulena had prophesied: a Greed King would transform the world with one, loving thought. I grabbed him by the chest of his space suit. I tossed him into the air, and lifted him high above my head.

Ulena had promised that a Greed King would transform the world when his own love of loving overtook him for one moment. Tronot was thinking before I grabbed him, "If only Janey and the kids could see this miracle of the awakening Sun Quartz Fields." He had forgotten his greed and his rage. Tronot's experiencing a moment of love was Earth's moment of salvation.

I continued to holding him high above my head with his face toward the Sun Quartz Fields. Nanu appeared, hugely before us, as I held Tronot. "Remember me, Memsek?" She said to him. His face twisted with fear and recognition. His ancient memories had been awakened by the power of the ignited Sun Quartz Fields, as had all of ours.

"Nanu!" Tronot shouted. "Nanu, I swear I've suffered through the ages for what I did to you. Please forgive me!"

Nanu smiled, her doe-eyes gentle. "I do forgive you, with all my heart. You have transformed Earth and allowed for this long-prophesied miracle. You are going to be set free, to live in perfect bliss among the Sun Quartz fields. Your heart will be cleansed as you live in bliss. Power has always been your greatest love, and now you will know ultimate power, as you energize the fields for a hundred years as a Light Being."

"Thank you," he whispered. I guess he knew he didn't have much choice, but his soul also seemed to recognize it would finally be set free from millennia of darkness.

"Open the door!" I shouted to some Greed King astronauts who were standing around with gaping mouths and rapture-filled faces. The bright happiness filling our ship—once a ship of darkness—was dizzying. Holding this man up high over my head, it was all I could do to keep from laughing with joy.

The astronaut thrust open the door. Below us, a long tunnel led right to the throbbing heart of the Sun Quartz Fields. Crazy pink light and love and joy blazed up at us through the tunnel from the brilliant Sun Quartz Fields below.

Feeling like Xena the Warrior Princess, I tossed Tronot down the tunnel. When he reached the center, another huge explosion of light blasted us, and all of us could feel his joy and love. Memsek-Tronot was free, and happy.

Nanu's beautiful face radiated joy when Memsek-Tronot reached the Sun Quartz Fields. She turned to me and smiled. "Finally, my Pepper, thanks to you and your bravery, I, too, am finally free." She hugged me hard, and before I could say anything, golden light flashed outside the ship. While Light Beings sang and danced joyfully about in the heavens, Caleina and Mother Ibis slowly flapped their wings outside the ship, looking deeply into our eyes.

Caleina nodded solemnly at me first, then at Nanu. Mother Ibis' wings grew brighter, and her look into my eyes was deep and loving. They beckoned Nanu with their bowed heads, and swooped toward the bottom of the tunnel. Nanu jumped down the tunnel, laughing and hollering like a young girl. She landed hard, onto Caleina's back, and laughed. Mother Ibis swept behind Caleina and Nanu. She looked up through the tunnel at me one last time, and her warm black eyes shone lovingly. I felt her love. The three of them then flew swiftly and joyfully into the heart of the Sun Quartz Fields. When their spirits hit the Fields, whitish-pinkish-purplish light blasted our ship. We all felt their massive, radiating joy and love.

Magically, the other astronauts inside the ship followed Tronot and Nanu. They jumped down the tunnel, singing and shouting, into the Sun Quartz Fields. Each time a new being reached the fields, light exploded, and loving joy burst into the atmosphere. I could feel it! It felt ten times bigger than the happiest ending possible in a movie. We were all crying with happiness.

The crews in Tronot's other ships, however, were not yet part of the miracle. Power still looked good to them, and, with all the commotion, easy. Out of nowhere, a missile suddenly fired from Omnipotence 3, and our ship bolted.

A huge, white star appeared suddenly outside, and swallowed the missile whole, the second before it would have hit our ship. The missile blasted, but was fully absorbed inside this brilliant star. Before our eyes, the "star" became King Kanta; white and firey, he belched a massive, firey belch.

"I've eaten nukes bigger than that for breakfast, down below in the sea," his voice boomed over the loudspeaker. He shouted at Tronot's other ships. "If you'd like to try another," he roared, "I swear, I'll spit it right back at you, at ten times the force, you tiny twits!"

Silence answered from Tronot's other ships.

When I returned to the cockpit, Butara was holding Marla. Her face radiated perfect joy, but she was dying.

"Butara, I thought we'd all be healed, like I was, at the time of the Awakening! I mean, look at me! I'm walking! Why didn't it work for Marla?"

"Tronot shot me before the Awakening, my dear, before the Universe was transformed with Light and Love. Besides, my purpose has been fulfilled. Thirteen millennia is a long time, Pepper," Marla said, smiling. She seemed so happy. She had no fear; after all, she had died a few times before.

"Marla, I could cure you! I have all the ancient healing ways from Makara within me. I know how to do that radiant healing thing from the head, like she does!" I shouted, and prepared myself to do it.

"No, no, Sweetheart." Marla held my hand to stop me. "I have been a Sea Faerie Keeper of Memories long enough."

Rona and Lillith appeared in the cockpit.

"Mother!" Marla said, smiling gently.

"Sweet Girl," Lillith cooed, "you've done this before. Lean toward the Light, and go home to God."

"Yes, Mama," Marla said, dreamily. She turned to Rona. "Can I be a dolphin, next time?"

Queen Rona smiled. "Of course, my Marla."

Rona and Marla began to laugh the tinkly, Koban laugh together. Liquid, neon colors swirled above their heads. Colors rioted through the ship, which was already blazing with pink light from the awakened Sun Quartz Fields.

King Kanta appeared with another belch. He looked ruffled, and his face was purple. His cloud of snowy white hair raged all around him. "Rona, my Queen, after we get the Kobans settled on the New Earth, and they help the humans adapt to life without suffering, what do you say we join Marla? We could have fun, being dolphins together." His arms swept around his queen.

Queen Rona smiled as she rubbed Marla's hand. While Lillith stroked Marla's hair, Rona said, "My sister, the Living Kuan Yin, can finally go home to heaven, for no longer will a single human suffer. I stayed because I was inspired by my sister's pledge, but you may have a point, my king. Just for fun! One more life, as a dolphin! Okay, we'll do it, Marla, dear." Rona leaned to speak into Marla's ear. "See you in the deep, blue sea, Girlfriend."

Marla turned to me and winked. "That awful language again. Pepper, I leave you with my powers and my pen. You are now the Keeper of Earth Memories."

With that, her body and face glowed brightly for an instant, and then she was gone. I watched in wonder, but was not sad. Marla's face smiled joyfully in sleep.

I humbly took the glowing, ceremonial pen from Marla, the Sea Faerie Keeper of Memories. She bestowed upon me a great honor, and I hope to someday write as well and sagely as she did.

Crewmembers from Tronot's five other ships came on the loudspeaker above the music and singing. One by one, they surrendered.

"We surrender all to the greater good," their spokesman said.

King Kanta towered fiercely over them. His ravaged face softened slightly. "An excellant choice. Peaceful Queen or not, I would have blown you all to smithereens!"

LIFE AFTER THE AWAKENING

From the Earth Memories Archives
Compiled by Pepper McCullah
Clan of the Fan-Feathered Brow
Earth Year 2031

My first clue to life after the awakening of the Sun Quartz Fields was when I didn't feel sad, losing Marla. Marla had risked her life for me, and had become a beloved friend. I'd wanted to save her, and I could have, using the ancient, healing technique, and knowledge left to me by my clan. She would not allow it. Rather than sadness, or frustration, I felt joy. The mission she trained for, for 13,000 years, was complete. She was home.

My whole being was filled with complete joy, around and through me. I felt loved, and connected, lovingly, to all living things: I was now a part of the Sun Quartz fields, and the Universe, and everything that sparkled in the sky, in the sea, or on land, at home. I almost felt my body could not contain my happiness.

Rona beamed at me, and the entire ship filled with Koban colors. Once again, she rejoiced. "My sister Kuan Yin says she is now going home to heaven, because there is no longer one human left suffering on Earth."

"Really?" I asked. It was too big a concept to grasp.

"You'll see. If you close your eyes, and think of the ones you love, back on Earth, you will know." With that, she kissed me on my forehead, and was gone in a flash of fuchsia-golden light.

In an instant, I was inside the Wisdom Palace with the other twelve Wheelchair Warriors. I felt their rapture. They'd done their jobs well. In my mind, I saw again what they'd experienced: thousands of jolts of purplish-pinkish, white-electric charges of energy that nearly killed them. They'd convulsed in their chairs as their bodies raged with electricity, which then shot downward from the breaks in their spines. Magically, I saw the blasts of energy surge and descend to the core of Earth. Once they had finished their journey, the electrical blasts returned to the Warriors' bodies, then surged upward, to circle the circumference of Earth.

I could feel the loving light energy they had surged with their bodies, minds, hearts, and spirits, deep into the core of Earth. I could feel the same surging light energy passing around Earth's circumference. I shouted for joy. "Way to go, Wisdom Retrievers!!!"

I then thought of my family on Earth, and felt my mother's tears of joy salt my face, just as my fans' tears of sorrow had once done. Everything was the biggest joy ever.

Butara appeared. "I feel a party comin' on. You did good, Football Girl. I see you won't need this anymore," he/she said and vaporized my wheelchair.

"There's a hockey dude who wants me to beam him up. You ready for that?" He asked.

"Heck, yes," I said, and poofo, Todd stood before me on his own two legs. His face was goofy with happiness, probably just like mine.

"Do you believe how good this is?"

"No," I said, and we hugged for a long time before Butara beamed him back into his own ship. I felt the connections as I held him: to his past, his clan, and to our future.

"See you back on Earth," I said telepathically to Todd.

We traveled five million miles in two or three days, I guess—who knows? I stayed full of bliss. I spent a lot of time just blissing: that is Zoloat for feeling joy beyond anything ever. I felt grateful, and loved by Creator and all creation. I was connected to all the ages, and all the spirits of those who'd lived in all the ages. The thought of humanity never suffering again was too big to grasp, but Butara assured me it was good.

Lounging hugely in the air above me, as if on a luxurious daybed, Butara told me, "Misery was seductive. Enough to have seduced humanity for tens of thousands of years, but you will be amazed by how much there is to do when you don't have tension, chaos, misery, and destruction. Look at you, Pepper McCullah! You just spent three days doin' nothin' but blissin'! It's a good time, I'm telling you. Zoloatons have been without misery and chaos for well over seventy thousand years, and we love it! We ain't never goin' back to the misery and chaos thing!"

Butara and I were alone in a ship that had carried so many more people to the Sun Quartz Fields. It was an honor to spend time with one so wise in ancient ways. He/she taught me how to guide humans toward using their powers of love in everything we do and create. "Begin with your planet. She needs healing, and you have the healing power passed down through your Clan. Nurture her, tend to her, and go from there. Earth will keep you busy awhile, but then, you can become caretakers for the lost planets, as Zoloatons have. Think about that! You may end up doing my job, someday, Football Girl: out there, in some distant, troubled galaxy."

I smiled at Butara's glowing, golden face. He knew something about my future. I shrugged and said, "What will be, will be. It's all good!"

My ship was first to land. Earth was different. A hundred Koban colors swooped up, arched, and intersected, filling the skies like fireworks above the Wisdom Palace. Ulena was there to greet us, and her silvery eyes now shone blue. She was healed, just as the Kobans had promised. Her face lit up when she saw me walk on my own two legs to her, and we held each other for a long time.

My parents' and brothers' faces glowed with bright grins. I'd never seen them look so happy! I realized how much we'd all been through together: many deaths, the near destruction of Earth, then life in the dark, throbbing womb of the Earth Core Tunnels, then my paralysis. That was enough! I knew, surrounded by my family in a group hug, that Butara was right: we would be just fine without chaos and misery for the rest of our lives!

Todd and Rakama's ship landed second, and he and I could not have been more joyful. We looked deeply into each other's eyes and stood, offering the palms of our hands to each other. I then slapped Todd like a dorky girl, and started playing a silly game of tag. Since we'd met, our biggest, secret wish had been to run together.

I sang, "You're it!" just so he would chase me. We laughed our heads off, running around, and joyful tears filled my father's eyes.

My dad is so cute! He'd brought a football to the homecoming of my ship! A great game of father-daughter pass ensued, and I was happy enough, I could have died right then and been okay with it. Mom and Grandma Sandy had their arms around each other, and they also could have popped, they were so happy.

The final ship of my crew landed, and Arinne, Tamdin, Micah, and Danu walked out on their own legs. We jumped up and down on our sturdy, new legs. We shouted and cheered, and we were all like shiny, new people who would spread massive joy and love everywhere.

Butara was right about the party. A great celebration began, all over the world. At this writing, the celebration continues: we dance, we sing, we laugh, and we love everything. We give thanks. The Sun Quartz Fields have surrounded our planet with a halo of light that fills our world with serenity, peace, and joy. There is never darkness, sadness, or lack of energy anywhere. Power is provided for by the dazzling Sun Quartz Fields, (and Tronot!), so nobody has to pay for it. There is no sickness that cannot be healed with love and light. All toxins can be whisked away by the heartfelt unity of heart-body-mind-and-spirit.

I celebrate all who have come before, and I celebrate all who brought us here. Their love, and their tremendous sacrifices through the ages have brought us to perfect joy, which was their intent. I love them for loving us!

I sign off for now. I nod my heart to Marla, the Sea Faerie Keeper of Memories. May you swim and laugh freely as a dolphin whose laughter will be heard in the distant cosmos. I remain always your friend and loving sister.

THE END

ABOUT THE AUTHOR

Reverend Pamela Camille has traveled five continents, studying the truth and spiritual wisdom of ancient cultures and their mythology. Graduating With Honors from Stanford University with a B.A. degree in English/Creative Writing, her minor field of study was cultural philosophy. *Awakening the Sun Quartz Fields* is the spiritual fruit of a lifetime of study and travel thrown in with her zesty love for sports and life and fun.

A published author in every genre for 24 years, her nonfiction book on child abuse, *Step on a Crack,* won praise from Oprah Winfrey. For eighteen years, she was the Contributing Editor for the International Literary Quarterly, *Crosscurrents,* and in that capacity, worked with globally renowned authors and poets. Her nonfiction book on financial abuse of the elderly, *Getting Older, Getting Fleeced* won her a post in the San Jose, California judicial system as an expert witness in trials against financial abusers of the elderly. She is proud she helped put looters behind bars. Her "fun book," *Your Auntie Wouldn't Lie: What the Other Baby Books Don't Tell You,* was a comic book about motherhood, her favorite, all-time occupation. She dedicated it to her many nieces and nephews.

Having meditated, studied, and prayed in ashrams, temples, and churches all over the world for decades, Reverend Camille now performs weddings on golden sands at Lake Tahoe. She lives in harmony and joy with her beloved husband and two sons in Zephyr Cove, Nevada, at Lake Tahoe.

0-595-31582-8